CINDERELLA WIFE

Susanna *knew* there was a mutual attraction, but when Davin refused to acknowledge it, how could she break down the barriers?

CINDERELLA WIFE

BY

KATHERINE ARTHUR

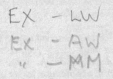

EX — LW
EX — AW
" — MM

MILLS & BOON LIMITED
ETON HOUSE   18–24 PARADISE ROAD
RICHMOND   SURREY   TW9 1SR

First published in Great Britain 1985
by Mills & Boon Limited

© Katherine Arthur 1985

Australian copyright 1985
Philippine copyright 1987
This edition 1987

ISBN 0 263 75589 4

Set in Linotron Times 10 on 11½pt.
05–0887–52,700

Photoset by Rowland Phototypesetting Limited,
Bury St Edmunds, Suffolk

Printed and bound in Great Britain by
Cox & Wyman Ltd, Reading

CHAPTER ONE

'YOU'RE fired!' Cyril Bostwick yelled, clutching his smarting cheek.

'Oh, no, I am not.' Susanna Blair turned and glared at the enraged director. 'I quit! My part is finished, and if you try to cut it out I'll sue!' With that she fled, slamming the door behind her.

It was a long, hot drive from the movie location in the Mojave Desert to Susanna's small apartment in Van Nuys, but it took the entire time for her to calm her seething anger, which was directed even more at herself than at the unfortunate Cyril Bostwick. 'You blew it. You let the situation get out of hand,' she berated herself over and over. If there was one thing Susanna had learned in her five years in Hollywood, it was to always stay one jump ahead of lechers like Cyril Bostwick. She should not have sat down next to him on that couch. She should have jumped up the moment she had an inkling of his intentions. But he was a famous director and she knew she had been good in her part. There was always that faint hope that this time might be different. 'Dummy,' she scolded. 'Big, stupid, foolish dummy!' Now she was out of work, and even though her part was completed in *Murder for Fun*, she knew it would be a while before she found another part. Cyril might not be able to really keep her off the screen for ever, as he had threatened, but he could make life difficult, that she knew. She doubted he would make good his threat to cut her part. The picture was already over budget, and he could ill explain reshooting the scenes she was in. Where she would get the money to sue if he tried it, she had no idea, but she had friends in the cast and she would know if he did and go to the top with her complaint. With Cyril's lurid reputation she had a good chance of making a case on her own behalf.

'I sure hope Sigmundsen's has a lot of work for me,' she thought with a grimace as she shouldered her tote bag and picked up her suitcase, climbing the outside staircase to the second story of the Spanish-style building where she lived.

'Susanna! Susanna!' There was a call from the courtyard below and a round-figured, dark woman appeared by the little fountain. 'Welcome home! Glad you're back. How did the movie go?'

'Pretty well,' Susanna answered. 'How's everything with you, Maria?' Maria Gonzalez and her husband managed and maintained the small apartment complex.

Maria shrugged expressively. 'Good as can be expected. Come have some coffee tomorrow morning and I'll tell you—I got to run now. But there's a message—call Sally Holbrook. She's tried all week to get you. I told her I didn't know when you'd be back, but she said she was *desperate* for you to come in. Anyway, you'd better call her. Okay?'

'Okay,' said Susanna with a sigh and a wave of her hand to Maria as she unlocked her door. She had wished for more work from Sigmundsen's, but not quite this soon. Sally Holbrook was manager of the couturier salon at the exclusive store where Susanna worked part-time, modelling and helping Sally arrange shows and deal individually with the many wealthy customers. A frantic call from Sally usually meant a special kind of customer, someone very, very rich from out of town, sometimes even a sheik or other royalty, usually very demanding, and Susanna was in no mood to cater to such a person on this particular afternoon. Reluctantly she sank into a chair and punched the number of the store.

'Hi, Sally,' she said when they had been connected. 'What's up?' The answer confirmed her suspicions.

'I've got a real live one coming in at four,' Sally chuckled in her husky voice. 'This guy's got more oil than a goose has feathers, and he wants nothing but the best for his *dahling* daughter. I know you must be bushed after just driving in from the desert, but I really need you. I really do.'

'Oh, Sally,' Susanna sighed, frowning and running her fingers through her hair, 'I just don't know . . . It's been a really dreadful day. I had a little run-in with Cyril and he fired me.'

'He *what*?' Sally's voice carried the image of her dramatically raised eyebrows, and Susanna smiled to herself at the mental picture.

'Yes . . . well, he couldn't, really, because my part was finished, but he offered to expand it and to "make me a great star" . . . mostly from a horizontal position, I'm afraid.'

'Oh, no!' groaned Sally. 'That nasty little lecher. I hope you told him off good and properly.'

'I'm afraid I did more than that. I was pushing him away, and I forgot I had on those false fingernails. They gave him quite a set of scratches on one cheek. He was absolutely furious!' Susanna went on to enumerate Cyril's threats, while Sally snorted indignantly in sympathy.

'Of all the nerve!' she cried when Susanna had finished. 'I don't blame you for being upset. Still, it might perk you up to come in to the store and play dress-up for a while, don't you think?' When Susanna did not respond immediately, she added in wheedling tones, 'Would double pay lure you in?'

'I guess it might at that,' Susanna admitted, the practical side of her mind remembering that she would have to eat for some time on what her job at Sigmundsen's might pay. 'Just give me time to shower and do my hair. I think I can make it by four.'

'Bless you!' chortled Sally in relief. 'I'll get everything lined up.'

In less than an hour Susanna was refreshingly showered, dressed in a light blue jumpsuit, and had her hair fluffed into the appropriate style. Another forty-five minutes and she was walking into the back door of the dressing room, where a long rack of clothing waited for her talent to display it to its best advantage.

'Wow!' Susanna gasped as she surveyed the collection. 'Doesn't the poor girl have anything to wear?'

Sally shrugged, throwing her arms wide. 'Who knows? What the man said was she needs a "compleeet wahrdrobe",' she said, imitating a Southern drawl. 'That ought to do it, don't you think?'

Susanna fingered through the different outfits, each set up with elegant accessories to match. 'Not much here I'd go for,' she said with a wry grimace.

'Neither would I,' agreed Sally with a grin, 'but not everyone has our elegant taste. My guess is that this is what the gentleman had in mind. And if that's his "daughter" with him,' she added cynically, 'I'll eat my Gucci shoes.'

'You're probably right.' Susanna sighed as she unzipped her jumpsuit and stood in front of the full-length mirror in her bra and bikini. 'I hope I haven't lost too much weight getting dehydrated in that desert.'

'You look terrific,' Sally told her in her frank and kindly way. 'If I had that body I'd be sitting out there with that fellow and not back here helping you dress.'

'You're not dumb enough,' said Susanna with a laugh. 'Now, where shall I start?'

For almost an hour Susanna worked her way through the assorted outfits, turning and smiling in the luxurious beauty of the mirrored salon, every move shimmering in multiple reflections, every sound hushed by the velvet draperies and thick carpets. In spite of the instant dislike she took to the overweight man who stared at her with cold and beady eyes, she put on her most winning smiles for him. If nothing else she would see that the poor frightened creature who sat beside him, obviously ill at ease in these rarefied surroundings, would have some really lovely clothes. Not the understatedly elegant garments that Susanna would have chosen, but excellent quality nonetheless.

The last dress Susanna was to model was an evening gown of black silk chiffon, daringly low-cut, adorned with layer upon layer of ruffles. The skirt was slit thigh-high on the side.

'This is really awful,' Susanna grimaced as Sally fastened an opulent diamond necklace on her and zipped up the back of the dress.

'Turn around and smile,' commanded Sally, and Susanna obeyed. 'Fantastic! I expect to hear you burst into a chorus of "Diamonds are a Girl's Best Friend" any minute.'

Susanna giggled. 'If I could sing I would. I wonder what our customer would think of that?'

'*If* you could sing like you can model he'd love it,' Sally declared. 'Now get out there and lay on the charm. It's getting late and I'm hungry.' In spite of her association with the wealthiest of the wealthy, Sally was always completely down-to-earth.

In front of the couple, who sat like monarchs on the opulent carved chairs with wine-red upholstery, Susanna paused and turned gracefully, smiling first at the portly gentleman and then at his companion.

'Oh, Daddy, I love it!' the girl breathed ecstatically, turning longing eyes from the dress to her friend.

'Come a little closer,' commanded the man, and Susanna obeyed. 'Are those real diamonds, little lady?'

'Yes, they are.'

The man nodded, his eyes in an appraising squint. 'I like it. I like the whole thing. We'll take one of those outfits for sure. Just waltz it around one more time, if you don't mind.'

'Of course,' Susanna said politely, smiling happily. At least the girl could hock the necklace if things didn't work out. She glided towards the draperies at the back of the room. There was a movement in the corner and, thinking it was Sally, Susanna impishly crossed her eyes and stuck out her tongue as her back was to the room. To her horror she immediately realised that the observer was not Sally, but Davin Sigmundsen himself, the austerely elegant owner of the store. Her head remained glued in a backward position as she turned, her eyes wide, as the towering figure of Davin Sigmundsen came into full view and he raised his eyebrows at her, his mouth quirked up at one corner in a reproving smile.

'Oh, lord, what have I done now?' Susanna groaned inwardly, jerking her head back to its proper position and reinstalling a smile on her face. She returned to pirouette again in front of the customers.

'Thank you, ma'am,' said the man, this time actually returning her smile, and Susanna nodded courteously and gracefully made her retreat. As she approached the dressing room door the curtains parted again and Davin Sigmundsen walked through the salon without a glance at her. She peeped out after making her exit. There was Davin Sigmundsen, exchanging a warm handshake with the customer.

'Oh, Sally, I've done it now!' Susanna wailed as she turned to be unzipped from her dress. 'If that man doesn't buy everything we showed him Mr Sigmundsen will think I fouled it up somehow.' She explained about her grotesque face.

Sally shook her head. 'Don't worry—Davin Sigmundsen might look like he's carved out of ice, but he's pretty reasonable. Besides, what harm is there in making a face behind someone's back? It's not as if you were doing it to offend them.'

'I know, but the way my luck's been today he's bound to think I was. I've already been fired once today. I think I'll just go home and hibernate for a week and see if things don't get better.'

'I don't blame you,' Sally said sympathetically, 'but don't count on taking a whole week off. We're short-handed right now, and I for one won't hear of your being fired. How about one day off?'

'How about two?' Susanna countered. 'One day to rest, and one to clean my apartment and do the washing.'

'It's a deal,' Sally replied, and Susanna beat a hasty retreat, not wishing to be there if Davin Sigmundsen came looking for her.

She had seen Davin Sigmundsen around the store often enough to know how swiftly he could pounce on any imperfections, his scathing comments slicing cruelly into any area manager he faulted. A perfectionist, she had heard, cold, calculating, and efficient. A miracle worker to those whom he praised, a man who had taken a stodgy store and built it to a pinnacle of chic. Susanna had never had a run-in with the man, nor any personal contact, but she had heard plenty. There were rumours about his wild youth, his transformation into a business genius, the many gorgeous women whom he wined and dined. But no big romances. There had been a brief flurry of news linking him with Margo Fanchon, the French actress, but she had married an Italian director and put an end to that. In general, the women pictured with him were wealthy or famous, seemingly chosen to enhance his image of perfection in this volatile, tinsel world. Susanna's heart sank as she realized the kind of image she must have created. Davin Sigmundsen would have little use for a model who clowned behind a customer's back.

Too exhausted and depressed to cook, she made a dinner of peanut butter sandwiches and milk and collapsed on her bed soon after, intending to sleep until she really felt like getting up. The ringing of her bedside phone wakened her, and as she fought off the fog of a still heavy sleep she saw that it was barely eight o'clock in the morning.

'Hello?' she said in a voice still thick with sleep.

'Miss Blair? Sorry to waken you.' The deep male voice sounded slightly sarcastic. 'This is Davin Sigmundsen. Would you mind coming to my office at ten o'clock? There's something I'd like to discuss with you.'

Susanna frowned at the telephone. So Davin Sigmundsen wanted her to jump out of bed and hurry to his office just so he could fire her! She was in no mood to rush like mad just to take part in that event. 'I can't make it by ten,' she said sulkily. 'How about eleven?'

There was a short pause. 'Very well, eleven. I'll see you then.'

'Very well, eleven,' Susanna mimicked back at the receiver as she put it down. 'Very well, indeed. I suppose it's some kind of honour to be fired by the owner instead of the personnel manager.' She padded barefoot into the bathroom and glared at her reflection in the mirror. Her eyes were puffy and her cheeks were pale, the strain of the previous day having taken a toll even though her spirit was undaunted. 'Ugh,' she muttered, sticking out her tongue and squinting at it. 'I could have used another ten hours of sleep.' She turned on the shower and watched absently as clouds of steam began to billow over the top of the door. Finally she slipped off her nightdress and adjusted the temperature, stepping in to let the warmth flow over her until she felt awake and alert.

After drying her hair with a vigorous brushing to straighten the luxurious waves, she slipped into her Oriental robe and made her way to her tiny kitchen. 'Let's see . . . coffee, bacon and eggs, toast and jam. No need to watch my weight for a while.' She was just sitting down to her repast when there was a knock on the door. It was Maria.

'Come on in,' Susanna invited. 'Have some of my coffee for a change. I've got to go in to Sigmundsen's in a little while to get fired.'

'You can't be serious!' Maria's dark eyes widened incredulously.

'Let me tell you about yesterday,' offered Susanna, placing a cup of coffee before Maria. Between bites of her breakfast she gave Maria the details of the disastrous day, interrupted frequently by Maria's exclamations of distress.

'Oh!' 'That terrible man!' 'You poor little thing!' 'I

can't believe it!' As Susanna concluded with the morning's call from Davin Sigmundsen, Maria wrung her hands and shook her head. 'The man must be a tyrant. What harm did you do, making a little face? I know you need the job, but you're better off not working for a beast like that. Nasty, disgusting old man!'

Susanna sighed. 'Actually he's not old, and he certainly doesn't look disgusting. I've never seen him up real close, but he's very tall and handsome from across the room. He's always being pictured with some gorgeous movie star on his arm.' She wrinkled her nose. 'He probably thinks he's God's gift to the women of the world. Well, I intend to give him a piece of my mind before I'm through.'

'And well you should,' Maria agreed with feeling. 'It's women letting men lord it over them that have made us subject to such disgraceful behaviour as that . . . Cyril displayed. You stand right up to Mr Sigmundsen. Don't let him scare you.'

'I won't,' Susanna promised, smiling to herself. Maria was forever marching for women's rights, but at home Tony, her husband, was definitely the boss, although a gentle one.

By ten-fifteen Susanna was dressed, her hair pulled back into a sophisticated chignon. The dress she had chosen was navy blue silk with a mandarin collar, the asymmetric closing in front trimmed with lime green. She carried a blue purse, her pumps were also dark blue. Her only jewellery was a pair of diamond stud earrings that her parents had given her. She looked more elegant and cool than she felt.

'Good,' she said to herself as she got into her car. 'I'm going to be a little late.' As she drove she rehearsed to herself the various possible retorts she would make when Davin Sigmundsen told her she was fired, discarding from consideration any that sounded shrewish or just plain childish. She decided on a chillingly refined contempt, verging on hauteur. 'Thank you, Mr Sigmundsen,' she said out loud. 'You don't know how pleased I am *not* to be working for a man as small-minded and petty as you are.' That was it!

The office of the owner and president was in a small wing extending to the back of the store, its wall of glass overlooking and enclosed patio where a fountain tinkled beneath a spreading live oak tree. As Susanna was ushered in by a severe-looking middle-aged woman, Davin Sigmundsen rose from his desk and came towards her. She would have liked to raised her chin defiantly, but his towering height made that impossible without breaking her neck, so she smiled faintly and said,

'I'm afraid I'm a little late.'

Instead of a frown, the response to her statement was a pleasant smile that revealed beautifully even teeth and deep smile lines around a pair of eyes that were a startling sea-green. It was easy to see why women were anxious to be seen in Davin Sigmundsen's company. His hair was a deep auburn, slightly curly, cut in the most fashionable style. His cheekbones were high and pronounced, his chin square and firm. The expensive grey suit, obviously tailored to his broad-shouldered, slim-hipped body, seemed deliberately understated, as if his tailor knew better than to try to compete with the drama of the man's naturally vivid colouring.

'It was worth the wait,' Davin Sigmundsen said surprisingly, in a deep, well-modulated voice, his eyes appreciative but not offensive as he looked at Susanna, a slight tension revealed in the lines about his eyes. It was

not a leer, but a look of carefully controlled appraisal.
He extended his hand. 'I'm sorry I haven't taken the
trouble to meet you before, Miss Blair. May I call you
Susanna?'

With a reflex of good manners, Susanna held out her
hand and found it engulfed in Davin Sigmundsen's large
one, which felt strong and calloused, more like the hand
of a labouring man than a desk-bound executive. Put off
her course by this friendly approach, she could only
shrug at his question. 'How tall are you?' she asked, the
words popping out before she could censor them.

At that Davin Sigmundsen smiled in amusement and
Susanna could not help but smile back, feeling a little
foolish. 'Six foot six, the last time anyone bothered to
measure,' he replied. 'Why?'

'I don't know, really,' Susanna laughed. 'Just curious.
I hope you're not offended,' she added, wondering to
herself why she should care, since she was still sure this
was not to be a pleasant occasion.

'Not at all.' Davin dropped her hand and gestured to a
chair by the side of his massive desk. 'Sit down, Susanna.
I have a business proposition to discuss with you.'

'A business proposition?' Her voice almost squeaked,
as she tried to rearrange her thoughts to allow for the
possibility that she was not going to be fired after all. She
sat in the indicated chair and studied Davin Sigmundsen
thoughtfully, a frown between her brows.

He returned her look, the intensity of his stare sending
a shiver of excitement coursing through her as their eyes
held for what seemed a long time. This was not the coldly
aloof Davin Sigmundsen that Sally referred to as the Ice
Man. She started at the sound of his voice as he repeated, 'Yes, a business proposition.' His eyes narrowed
shrewdly as he glanced away and then gave Susanna a

sideways look. 'Nothing like that little curve that poor Cyril threw at you yesterday.'

She gasped. 'How did you . . . ?' How could the news have spread so fast?

Davin looked at her directly. 'Sigmundsen Enterprises owns a controlling interest in Futura Pictures. Cyril came pounding on my door last night, demanding to be allowed to reshoot several scenes. I think you know why . . . and so did I as soon as I saw his face in the light. I told him what the producer had already told him . . . absolutely no. Well, aren't you pleased to hear that?' he asked as Susanna continued to stare at him, open-mouthed.

'I . . . er . . . yes. Yes, of course. I didn't expect to be cut, but I thought I might have to fight for it.'

'I'd hate to take you on,' Davin said dryly, 'after what you did to Cyril.'

'He deserved it,' Susanna snorted, 'and more! That little weevil ought to be . . .' She stopped, blushing.

'I get your drift.' Davin chuckled briefly, a deep throaty sound that she found surprisingly warm and appealing. He immediately became serious again. 'I'm afraid the job I have in mind for you is a little unconventional, but I assure you there is nothing immoral or improper involved.' He looked at her, a little anxiously, she thought, and a frown again creased her brow. Strange things did go on in Hollywood, but she had been there long enough so that very little surprised her any more. Nevertheless she was totally unprepared for Davin's next statement.

'I'd like to hire you to play the part of my wife for a short time. Probably about a year.'

'You *what*?' Susanna's voice rose shrilly. 'After what happened to me yesterday, you have the nerve to . . .'

She fairly jumped to her feet. 'I suppose you think that because you're the *owner* of Futura Pictures and the *owner* of this store . . . and tall and handsome . . . that I'll do for you what I wouldn't do for Cyril? Well, think again!' She whirled and marched towards the door, but before she had taken three steps a large hand clamped down on her shoulder.

'Hold on, Susanna, please. Hear me out. This is strictly a business proposition, as I said before.' He emphasised the word strictly, his face grimly serious as he turned her to face him. 'It would be a real marriage, but it would not be . . . consummated, or however you want to put it. I simply need to have a wife for . . . a very good reason.' His eyes were the deep green of a stormy sea as he peered into Susanna's face and she felt herself tremble at the intensity of his expression. Why should this handsome, wealthy man be turning to her, of all people? His suggestion was ridiculous, out of the question. He must know that.

'Mr Sigmundsen,' Susanna said, shaking her head as much in amazement as rejection, 'marriage of convenience went out with high buttoned shoes. I'm afraid you're a bit out of date.'

'Really? I think not.' He impaled her again with his penetrating stare. 'Think of the girls who marry for money, the boys who marry the boss's daughter, the student who marries to get a wife to put him through school, the actress who marries the producer. From my point of view, those are merely less honest versions, where the marriage is as doomed as if some contract were scheduled to run out.' He raised his eyebrows as if waiting for her reaction.

Susanna bit her lip. He did have a point, but . . . 'Why me?'

'Well, will you sit down again?'

'I guess so,' she said brusquely, sitting stiffly in her chair.

Davin Sigmundsen's mouth was set in a tight line as he rubbed his chin, appearing to be sorting out how best to approach her. Tense lines etched about his eyes, an inward-turned look darkening the deep green colour almost to black. 'Why you?' he said thoughtfully. 'Some very practical reasons, and others more personal.' He looked at her intently, as if by sheer force of his will he could make her agree to his logic, so that Susanna clasped her hands together tightly in front of her in a protective gesture against the onslaught of a powerful force.

'You have a promising career under way,' he went on, 'a career you would be eager to return to when the year was up. Also, as an actress, you should be able to do a convincing job of playing the adoring wife. Cyril admitted you had real talent in spite of your "stupid morality", as he called it.'

At this Susanna's frown darkened, but she remained silent.

'Another practical reason,' Davin went on, 'is my grandmother, who makes her home with me. She knows why it would be . . . convenient for me to marry soon, and would be suspicious if I were to marry one of the women she knows I've dated recently. I have not expressed any great admiration for any of them.' He paused and looked expectantly at Susanna.

'It's important to deceive your grandmother?' Susanna's tone was cold.

'I know it sounds unpleasant,' said Davin, his expression unhappy, 'but I'm afraid it's the only way. At her age she would never agree with my methods, no matter how worthy she might think my cause.'

'How worthy is it?' Susanna asked, her scepticism obvious.

'Very,' Davin replied, not going into any further detail. He leaned earnestly across his desk towards her. 'I thought it might appeal to you as an acting job, if nothing else. But judging from the sour look on your face, playing the part of my wife for a year would tax your acting skills to the utmost.' He cocked an expressively knowing eyebrow at Susanna, who was still regarding him soberly. 'I could help your career along quite a bit afterwards,' Davin went on, 'or hinder it.'

At this Susanna's eyes flashed. 'I wouldn't give in to blackmail yesterday, Mr Sigmundsen,' she snapped, 'and I'm not about to today, not even if I have to spend the rest of my life as a schoolteacher in Iowa.' She started to rise again, but Davin waved for her to sit, one hand rubbing his eyes.

'I'm sorry,' he said, 'that was stupid of me. I'm too used to dealing with people who'll do anything for a dollar or a part.' He smiled crookedly. 'Please forgive me. Of course, I would help your career. And the personal reasons I have for choosing you include the fact that you are a highly honourable person. I admired your response to Cyril, and Sally Holbrook told me what a fine young woman you are. She said you thought I might be upset about your making that face.' He smiled more broadly this time. 'In the circumstances I thought it was very appropriate.'

Susanna relaxed just a little, sinking back into her chair reluctantly. 'I don't know, Mr Sigmundsen . . .'

'Davin.'

'Er . . . yes, Davin.' Susanna pulled fretfully at the tip

of her nose. 'I'd have to know more about what would be expected of me.'

'Oh, just play the adoring wife whenever there's anyone around. I go out and entertain quite a bit, but I'm known as a rather . . . restrained person, so you wouldn't be required to fawn all over me. And of course, you'd have all the luxuries that I have to offer—a beautiful home, servants, that sort of thing. Plus a large salary of your own, to do with as you wish.' He leaned towards her. 'I'd see that it was a very pleasant year for you.' His face was earnest, almost pleading.

'Why?' she asked. 'Why do you need a wife so badly right now?'

As if a shutter had closed, Davin's face became an impassive mask. 'It's not something I can discuss with you at the moment.'

Susanna stared into space, her mind in a whirl. Never in her wildest dreams had she expected a proposition like Davin's. What would it be like to live, if only for one year, as one of the super rich? If only for one year . . . and when that year was up, just like Cinderella, her jewelled coach would turn back into a pumpkin. She could picture the elation of her parents at her marriage to this incredibly rich and handsome man, and their bitter disappointment when the marriage supposedly 'failed'. Could she carry that off? Would it be worth it to deceive them? The thought made her heart feel heavy within her, and she stood up to begin her habit of pacing while she thought out a problem.

'Susanna . . .' Davin began, but she looked at him sharply for a moment and pointed her finger at him.

'Just stay there,' she ordered peremptorily. 'I like to walk while I think.' She walked over to the wall of glass, staring blankly out at the beautifully manicured scene.

The perfection of the small palms, the unreal brilliance of the tuberous begonias, the painted emerald of the dichondra all looked like a part of the dream she felt she was having, a dream that included the possibility of spending a year in the company of a man whose physical beauty matched that of any leading man in Hollywood. A man who, she found herself admitting without a qualm, appealed to her as a person. He seemed honest, the motive which propelled his need for a wife apparently something of deep significance, if she were any judge. There was a man of strong passions behind that carefully controlled exterior, Susanna guessed. It would be interesting, perhaps even a little dangerous, to know him better. The thought made her shiver. His word would be her only guarantee that the marriage would be strictly business; there was no way she could fight off a man the size of Davin Sigmundsen if he determined to have his way with her. Could she trust him? She was inclined to think so, but . . .

Squeezing her chilly fingertips with first one hand and then the other, she began a circuit of the room, completely unconscious of Davin's eyes constantly upon her. She paused and stared at the pictures on the wall. They were as vivid and striking as the man behind the desk, one a seascape with children playing on the sand, another a woodland scene. The signature was D. Sigmundsen.

'Did you do these?' she asked, turning to face him.

He nodded and gave a self-deprecatory shrug. 'I used to paint a bit. Do you like them?'

'Very much,' she said, returning to her pacing. Similar tastes, her mind noted, her eyes sweeping from the pictures to take in the comfortably soft leather sofas, the warm colours. Perhaps his home would be to her liking too. She retrieved her mind from that tack, wondering why it acted as if she were actually going to see Davin's home when she had far from decided to take him up on his unusual offer. Unusual. That was just the trouble. Why did he need a wife? It must be something very important, perhaps illegal, that would drive him to such an extreme solution. It was obvious that Davin was a highly competent businessman, used to taking command. Susanna doubted that he was often involved in situations that were beyond his control. His wealth, plus his intelligence and charm, would prevent that. Charm. Yes, he did have that, although not the oozing, insincere kind that she detested. 'Darling little Susanna.' How she hated that approach! Davin had tried so hard not to offend her, to make her feel his need . . . She paused, back near his desk again, and looked at him. Their eyes met, neither of them flinching, but some kind of current of understanding passing between them. 'He has to trust me, too,' Susanna thought. 'I wonder how he can be sure he can? But then he hasn't told me . . .' She seated herself gracefully as years of drama classes had taught her to do.

'You'll have to tell me why you need a wife,' she said quietly. 'If I'm to trust you that this will be a strictly business arrangement, if I'm to deceive my friends and family, all of whom will assume my marriage is permanent, I have to know all of the details.' She folded her hands in her lap, her eyes fixed seriously on the handsome man before her. 'Frankly, I think I'm crazy even to consider it.'

Davin chewed his lip, his face troubled. 'I really can't,' he said slowly, his voice low. 'I'd like to, but you see, once I do . . .' He stopped and began again. 'It's like this. The problem that my marriage will solve is very personal. I can assure you that it's nothing dark or terrible, only rather sticky. Actually,' he paused and smiled warmly at her, 'it's something I'm sure you would approve of, something that will help someone else a great deal.'

Susanna shook her head. 'Davin,' she said seriously, 'surely you can see my point of view. What you suggest is highly unusual. For a man like you to have to hire a wife is . . . almost unbelievable. I just can't do it unless I know why I'm doing it. If you can trust me with the information later you can trust me with it now. I think,' she said, her blue eyes twinkling a little into Davin's green ones. 'That just like a real marriage, this one will have to be based on mutual trust or it won't work.'

'I can't tell you now.' Davin's voice was coldly positive. 'It seems to me that isn't asking too much in the way of trust either.'

'I'm afraid it is.' Susanna stood up. 'Goodbye, Mr Sigmundsen. I'm sure you'll be able to find someone else who'll be only too willing to take on your job. Why don't you try the casting agencies?' She smiled briefly, then turned to leave.

'It's you I want, damn it!' His voice was harsh. 'You're the first girl I've seen that I . . . who looks right. And for some reason, which I can't fathom at the moment, I think I could put up with your company for a year.' He half rose from his chair and then sat down again. 'Your decision is final?'

There was something about the querulous, almost little-boyish way he asked the question that made her smile, even as she nodded. 'Yes, it is. But if it's any comfort to you I think I could stand your company too, even though I don't quite know why.'

Davin rubbed his fist across his eyes, then ran his fingers repeatedly through his dark reddish hair, a picture of agitation that tugged at Susanna's sympathetic heart. If he would only at least give her a hint . . .

'All right.' He jerked his head up, his eyes staring piercingly at her as if trying to see into her head to confirm his decision. 'Sit down. I'll tell you. If,' he added as she sat once again, 'if you'll take the job when I do. This is not something I want in the papers.'

'Well,' Susanna began, biting her lip, 'I will unless your reason is something I thoroughly disapprove of.'

'It won't be.' Davin's mouth was set in a grim line. It was his turn to get up and pace across the floor, untying his necktie and tearing it off as he did so, tossing his jacket on to another chair, unbuttoning several buttons of his shirt. Then, seemingly more comfortable and, Susanna thought, decidedly more appealing, he sat down in his large swivel chair again and turned towards her.

'I need a wife so that I can take over guardianship of my ten-year-old nephew Bobby. When my brother Carl and his wife Elena were killed in an automobile accident over a year ago, Elena's parents took Bobby home with them. They've refused to give him up, even though I'm much better able to provide for him than they are. I've finally persuaded them, though, that it would be best—if and when I have a wife. I have it in writing, for whatever that's worth coming from them.' Davin scowled as he said this last.

Susanna was puzzled. 'But I should think his grandparents would be very suitable to bring up the boy. It's not as if he couldn't have the benefits of your money without living with you. Are you sure he'd want to leave them? I mean, it seems to me that you should consider his emotional needs as well as whatever needs money can provide for.'

'That's just what I am considering,' Davin said sadly. 'I didn't know Elena's parents well, and at first I thought as you do. I sent them extra money to take care of the expense of having another child to care for, but when I went to visit several times just to see how they were getting along I was . . . well, to put it kindly, appalled. The first time I found them both drunk, in the middle of the day. They weren't sure where Bobby was. When he did show up, he was filthy and dressed in clothing the Salvation Army wouldn't take as a gift. His "room" that he showed me was hardly any bigger than a closet. They had him sleeping on an old army cot, surrounded by empty beer cases. Naturally, I raised a ruckus about what I saw and they promised faithfully to correct the problems. I didn't have much hope that they would, but there wasn't much else I could do. Legally they have as much right or more to Bobby than I do. Then . . .' he sighed deeply, 'when I went back and found nothing was any better I lost my temper.'

'I don't blame you!' Susanna interjected, horrified at the picture that was forming in her mind.

'Yes . . . well, I shouldn't have. It just made things more difficult for Bobby. He cried that he wanted to come with me, they screamed and swore that he never would. It took me a couple more visits to get things calmed down so that we could talk reasonably.' He rubbed his neck wearily. 'I think the old lady really does love Bobby. She's the one who's stubborn about giving him up. The grandfather would do it in two seconds, for a price. Grandma Winters will only do it if Bobby will have someone to mother him—plus a price.'

'Why, that's blackmail!' Susanna protested. 'Can't you charge them with that?'

Davin shook his head. 'Not without a nasty court scene that I don't want Bobby involved in. Imagine the publicity over that one!'

'Mmmm.' Davin was right, Susanna thought, that she did understand and approve of his motive, except . . . 'Davin, one thing worries me,' she said thoughtfully. 'Won't having a mother who disappears after a year be worse than not having one at all?'

'It's far from an ideal solution,' Davin admitted. 'If there were another answer I'd certainly take it. But I guess I'm one of the unlucky ones where romance is concerned. I've only come close to marrying once, and then someone else stole her right from under my nose.'

'Could that have been Margo Fanchon?' Susanna wondered. She clucked sympathetically. 'Me, too. The captain of my high school football team. I thought the sun rose and set with him. Then phttt! Off he went with Mary Louise Crenshaw.' She smiled impishly. 'I saw her last summer, and she's already gained fifty pounds. I was just tickled to death to see that.' She paused and raised her eyebrows questioningly at Davin. 'Now that you know what a mean, petty person I am, do you want to change your mind?'

'Good lord, no,' Davin replied emphatically. 'I would have felt the same way.' He leaned towards her, a hopeful smile on his face. 'How about it? Will you do it?'

'I . . . I guess so. Yes,' Susanna said slowly, but as Davin's smile widened, she frowned. 'But we'll have to deal with the problem of Bobby's feelings very carefully. I don't want to do more harm than good.'

'You won't,' Davin said confidently. 'If you could . . . when you see the situation you'll feel that way too.'

'From what you said, I probably will,' she agreed with a grimace. 'Is this going to be a regular contract? I mean, do I sign up for exactly one year and then poof! Back to my cinders? It seems to me, considering Bobby, that it might be better to play it by ear. What do you think?'

'I think you're right. But I don't want to keep you away from your career for too long. That wouldn't be fair, just when you're getting a good start.'

Susanna reached over and placed her slender hand on Davin's arm. 'I'm not worried about that. When I take on a job I always try to do it right. But I'll try not to burden you with my presence for too long.' She smiled teasingly and received a warm smile in return, a smile that brought an unaccountably light and happy feeling to her heart.

'It won't be a burden. Well now,' he went on, becoming more businesslike immediately, 'how shall we do this? A whirlwind courtship and then a wedding in a couple of weeks?'

A couple of weeks! Susanna swallowed hard and rubbed her chin. In two weeks she would be Mrs Davin Sigmundsen! She must be losing her mind! 'That sounds fine,' she answered in a tiny, thin voice.

'Scared?'

'Mmm-hmm—terrified. "Can a girl from a small town in Iowa succeed as the wife of one of America's richest men?" I can see the headlines now.'

Davin laughed, a deep, throaty sound that sounded rich and masculine. 'You'll do wonderfully well. But let me assure you that I'm not "one of America's richest men". At least not in the top ten.'

'That's a relief,' Susanna replied, smiling. Then she added, as the thought occurred to her, 'Oh, dear, poor

Sally—she was counting on me to model. I don't suppose I'll be able to do that, will I?'

'Not after the wedding. But you might do some before, if necessary. It would look best that way. We've got to make this look like a genuine romance. Which reminds me, we might as well get started. How about having lunch with me in some nice conspicuous place?'

'Oh, no!' Susanna stiffened, her nerves suddenly tingling with anxiety. 'I mean, I'm not ready to begin right this minute. I need some time to get used to the idea . . . to convince myself that I'm not crazy.' She looked pleadingly at Davin. 'Can't I have until tomorrow?'

He scowled and then opened his mouth as if to speak in anger. Just as quickly he clamped it shut and took a deep breath. 'I forget the idea is much newer to you than it is to me,' he said, apologising for his unspoken words, for he had seen the anxious look come into her eyes. 'How about dinner tonight, then? But in some quiet place, down by the beach. You can wear your jeans, we'll go walking along the shore. Sound better?'

'Much better.' Susanna smiled a little tremulously, but with a comfortable feeling beginning to steal in to replace her fears. Davin was certainly understanding! He seemed as able to read her as she felt she could him. That should make it much easier for them to get along. She got to her feet, uncertain as to how she should make her exit. 'I'll see you later, then,' she said. 'Do you know where I live?'

'I know.' Davin got to his feet then and escorted Susanna to the door, his arm around her shoulders, his height making her feel almost Lilliputian. Before opening the door he stopped and quickly pulled her into his arms. Startled, she looked up and he bent his head and kissed her lips, very softly, very briefly.

'You're going to have to learn not to flinch when I kiss you,' he warned in a teacherly fashion.

'Hmmph,' she sniffed. 'If you kiss me like that, everyone will think I'm your sister.'

'Oh, really?' One corner of Davin's mouth quirked upward in amusement, and he swiftly lowered his head and proceeded to kiss her again. This time his lips were hotly insistent, demanding a response, yet gentle and tantalising as Susanna found it incredibly easy to surrender to the feeling of being totally mastered, enclosed, in the warmth of Davin's arms, her lips enjoying meeting their master and responding eagerly. Recognising the warning signs of the road to surrender, she pulled back and Davin offered no resistance as he released her.

'Better?' he asked with the lazily insolent look of a man certain of his powers to seduce.

'So much for stuffiness,' Susanna thought, wishing her heart would stop thumping so loudly. 'Much better,' she managed to reply tartly. 'We should be able to be quite convincing—without much practice.'

At this Davin threw back his head and laughed heartily. 'I like you, Susanna,' he said as he opened the door for her. 'I'll see you tonight.'

CHAPTER TWO

SUSANNA sat at the little round table in her apartment kitchen, staring blankly at the glass of tea before her. An after-shock of her decision had hit her and with it a sort of terror, a primitive desire to flee that her rational mind was trying to squelch. It was undoubtedly one of the crazier decisions she had made in her twenty-five years, ranking right up there with the impetuosity of her sudden move to California when her high school romance died on the vine. She had been going to finish college and get work as an English and drama teacher in some quiet little Iowa town. Then it had been anger and bitterness that had driven her, carefully concealed under a cheery bravado. 'I'll never know what I could have done if I don't try,' she had told her anxious parents. But what was motivating her now? Was it revulsion at Cyril's advances, at the knowledge that she would have to work ten times as hard if she declined all such invitations in the future? Not really, she thought, for work had never daunted her. More likely it was the novelty of the idea, for Susanna had never lacked for a spirit of adventure, and the year as Davin Sigmundsen's wife would be that.

But it was more than that, Susanna admitted to herself as she thought back to her hour in Davin's office. Davin Sigmundsen was a most intriguing and attractive man. 'Restrained,' he had described himself, but when he had talked of his nephew his expression had been that of a man who cares deeply and passionately. And that second kiss had been anything but restrained! Was his usual coolly aloof demeanour only a shield protecting a nature that was, perhaps, too passionate? Susanna shivered a little at the thought. That could be dangerous in a relationship such as theirs was to be. But doubtless Davin knew his weaknesses and would guard against them carrying him past the lines he had so clearly marked. And Susanna had best keep the rules in mind, too. Their 'marriage' was just a job, and she must never get carried away with the notion that she was a permanent part of Davin's exotic world. At least not yet. She still had hopes of making her way into that world on her own, on her talents and merit as an actress.

'Think now as an actress,' she instructed herself, rising from the table and beginning to pace about her small apartment, absently putting things to rights as she did. 'I am now a young lady who has had a most pleasant interview with Mr Davin Sigmundsen. Why did he want to see me, if not to fire me? I shall say it was to model a new collection, something that would take more time than I usually put in. Yes, that's it. And he was *sooo* nice—very handsome. And he invited me to go out with him tonight to talk about it some more. Just a casual dinner, nothing fancy.' Susanna smiled to herself as she worked her way into the part. It wouldn't be easy, she thought, pretending to fall in love with Davin, to be swept off her feet. She would have to be very careful with what she said, even to old friends like Maria. No one must ever guess the truth. At that thought she laughed out loud. The truth was so unbelievable that it would take a witch doctor to think of it! She went into her bathroom and stared in the mirror. 'I am a young lady who just met a fascinating, intelligent, charming, handsome gentleman, one with whom I could very easily fall in love,' she said to her reflection, taking her hair down and fluffing it with her fingers. A lovely, starry-eyed blonde girl, a pretty flush in her cheeks, stared back at her. 'My goodness, I am really quite an actress,' she breathed softly, a smile dimpling her cheeks. There was a knock on the door.

'Well, did you put that tyrant in his place?' Maria demanded the moment Susanna opened the door.

'I didn't have to! Come in and let me tell you all about it,' Susanna said vivaciously. 'He wasn't angry with me at all! He wants me to model a special collection. Isn't that fantastic?'

'Ah! How wonderful! But I'm not surprised,' Maria beamed. 'He must like a girl with some spirit. Not such a tyrant after all, then?'

'Oh, no! He was just as nice as could be. He even asked me out tonight to discuss it some more. Nothing fancy, though. He told me to wear jeans.' Susanna smiled in a prettily flustered way. 'He's really handsome, and very tall.'

Maria smiled knowingly. 'Something interesting is in the wind, in the sparkle in your eyes. Are you sure he only wants to talk business tonight?'

'Oh, Maria!' Susanna shook her head and frowned. 'I'm not in Mr Sigmundsen's league at all. He only dates really big stars and high society girls. Don't go getting any wild ideas.'

'I'll get all the wild ideas I like,' Maria replied good-naturedly. 'But this one is not, I think, so very wild.'

When Maria had gone, Susanna sank down on her couch and took a deep breath. Act One had gone rather smoothly. She had certainly given Maria the right ideas, and Maria had fallen for it hook, line and sinker. But then Maria was hopelessly romantic, even if she did know Susanna fairly well. All the same, not a bad beginning.

Susanna was still drying her hair when a firm knock on the door announced Davin's arrival. She slipped on her robe and hurried to answer it.

'Sorry I'm so early,' Davin apologised as he stepped in and closed the door behind him. 'I realised I hadn't told you what time I'd be here and I didn't want to keep you waiting.'

Susanna stared at him. He looked even more handsome than before, if possible, dressed in a short-sleeved madras plaid shirt and beige cotton slacks, white deck shoes on his feet. He looked quite elegant, but . . .

'I thought you said for me to wear jeans,' Susanna said, cooking her head questioningly.

He shrugged. 'Whatever is comfortable for you. I just meant to imply something casual.'

'Mmm, I see,' she said, mentally sorting through her wardrobe for a suitable outfit. Jeans were so much easier.

'You don't approve of my apparel.' Davin's mouth quirked into a half smile as he made the interpretation of her thoughtful stare.

'Well, if you must know . . .' Susanna paused briefly, then plunged ahead. If she was going to live with this man for a year . . . 'You look like something out of one of those sportswear catalogues,' she said pertly. 'You know, "what *everyone* is wearing to the shore this year" sort of thing. Don't you ever wear jeans?'

Davin almost choked on his laughter. 'Your little set-to with Cyril should have warned me that you don't pull your punches! Now I'm going to feel selfconscious all evening.'

'I'm sorry,' Susanna said contritely. 'You look very nice, really. I don't know why I said that.' Yes, she did, though, she thought. It had been a reflexive desire to break past that polished, cool image.

'Your delightful honesty,' Davin answered for her. 'It's a most appealing trait, and one I've not noticed in too many women.'

'It could also be called tactlessness,' Susanna said with a grimace. 'And I'm being rude, keeping you standing here.' She took his arm. 'Do come and sit down and have a drink while I get dressed.' She led him into her freshly sparkling little living room with its white-painted rattan furniture, the bright chintz cushions and banks of plants near the windows giving it the airy look of a garden.

Davin sank into the deep, cushioned armchair and stretched his long legs out on the ottoman in front of it with a sigh. 'This is a lovely room,' he said, looking around him with approval.

'I'm going to miss it,' Susanna admitted a little sadly as she poured a tall, cool drink. 'I've been here three years.' She handed the drink to Davin. 'But then I've always known it wouldn't be for ever.' She excused herself to go and get dressed, but as she was almost out of the door, Davin called out, 'Susanna!' and she stopped and turned to look at him.

'Wear your jeans?'

'I was going to,' she replied with a grin, and went quickly to her room. She put on a pair of well-washed jeans, a loose-fitting white cotton blouse, and leather sandals. In minutes she was ready, her hair brushed back and held with a headband, only a slight touch of mascara and lip-gloss for make-up.

The car to which Davin led her was a black Mercedes, exactly, she mused, the kind of car she would have expected the 'stuffy' Davin Sigmundsen to have. She wondered, as she fastened her seat-belt and Davin steered the car into the stream of freeway traffic, what kind of car Davin's alter ego would drive.

'Have you ever driven a Ferrari?' she asked.

'I used to have one,' he answered with a sideways glance at her. 'Why? Doesn't this car suit you? It's much more practical.'

'I was just curious,' Susanna replied. 'I like this one just fine. As far as I'm concerned, cars are just to get you someplace.'

Davin raised an eyebrow, looking at her sceptically. 'I find that hard to believe.'

'Why?' Susanna turned a wide, blue-eyed stare in Davin's direction. 'Having a particular kind of car can't make you something you aren't.' She looked thoughtful. 'But when you can afford any car you want, the one you choose does tell something about you.'

'Aha!' said Davin, smiling to himself, a little grimly, Susanna thought as she looked at his profile.

'I didn't mean . . .' she began, but Davin interrupted her.

'I know exactly what you meant,' he said dryly, ma-noeuvring the Mercedes expertly to take an off ramp. He pulled into the parking lot of a large shopping centre and soon found a space to park. 'Wait here. I'll be right back,' he ordered, and Susanna watched him stride swiftly away, a puzzled frown on her face.

'I've been tactless again,' she thought unhappily. She had better curb her tongue, or she would be out of this strange job before it had ever begun. But maybe that would be just as well. If Davin couldn't take her the way she was when they were alone . . . she certainly wasn't going to act *all* the time for a whole year!

When Davin returned a short time later, she stared at him in astonishment. Gone was his natty outfit, and in its place some pre-washed jeans, a knit shirt in white with gold and blue stripes edging the deep vee neck, and dark blue canvas shoes.

'Shall we stop and get a Ferrari now?' asked Davin with a grin, as she continued to stare at him in speechless wonder.

'Good heavens, no!' she cried out in horror. 'You didn't . . . you don't . . . I didn't mean for you to . . .'

'Oh? I was under the impression that you were a girl who said what she meant, even if it was tactless.'

Susanna reddened in embarrassment. 'Expressing an opinion isn't the same thing as giving orders, you know,' she grumbled. 'You don't have to go to extremes.'

'I was just trying to please you,' Davin protested mildly.

'Well, don't,' Susanna snapped. 'I've learned my lesson. I'll never open my mouth again.' She glared as Davin roared with laughter.

'I'll believe that when elephants roost in trees,' he chuckled. 'Tch, tch, here we are, having our first lovers' quarrel!'

'We're not lovers,' Susanna said acidly, 'nor ever likely to be. I can certainly see now why no woman would marry you.'

'Quite the contrary,' said Davin as he started the car and headed back towards the freeway. 'I've had several offers.'

'I should have said no woman in her right mind,' Susanna muttered.

He stared straight ahead. 'Do you want out of our contract?'

'No. Do you?'

'No. Why not?'

'Darned if I know,' Susanna replied, studying his strongly chiselled profile. 'Stubborn, I guess.'

'I'm *never* that way.' Davin's voice was positive.

'Why, you're . . .' she began, jerking her chin up to begin a contradiction. She stopped abruptly as he turned his head to look at her, his eyes twinkling mischievously. She subsided into helpless giggles. 'You remind me of my brother Jeff,' she said, wiping her eyes.

'Tell me about him,' Davin suggested, beginning to quiz her about her childhood in Iowa, listening with apparently intent interest as she told him of life in a small rural town, summers on her grandparents' farm, of toughening up under the teasing of two older brothers who alternately doted on her and considered her a pest.

'Why did you ever leave?' asked Davin, his voice wistful.

Susanna looked at him in surprise. 'You sound a little envious,' she said, and he nodded. 'It probably sounds better than it was,' she comforted. 'Besides, I had to see what I could do as an actress. At least I thought I did, after Darrell and I broke up. I couldn't see myself sitting around licking my wounds and waiting for whoever was second in line to show up.'

'You still seem more like an Iowa girl.'

'Oh, I am! I don't fit in with the swinging singles set at all, but I don't care. I'm not here to be everyone's favourite bedmate. I go to parties when it's necessary, try to be at least nice to the right people. I've made a few friends, but no one really close. Maria, who manages my apartment building, is probably the closest.' Susanna giggled. 'Not exactly the standard prescription for success, is it?'

Davin turned his head and smiled at her. 'It succeeds

with me. It sounds very much like we're two of a kind. My closest friend is captain of a fishing boat. He's intelligent enough to have done anything he wanted with his life, and that's exactly what he is doing.'

'And you're not?' Susanna had caught a regretful note in his voice.

'Only sometimes.'

She studied the profile of the huge man beside her. There was a tension in the firm jawline, in the lines that creased across his high cheekbones from the corners of his eyes. 'This pseudo-marriage can't be just what you've always wanted,' she said softly, and saw the tension relax as Davin reached over and squeezed her hand.

'I think it's going to turn out far better than I ever dreamed,' he said. 'Besides, Bobby means a great deal to me. More than anything I want to have him home with me.'

They drove in silence for a while, Susanna lost deep in thought. It was a little unusual for a man to care so deeply for his nephew, unless he and his brother had been unusually close. So far, Davin had said little about his brother. Perhaps the hurt of losing him was still too deep and sensitive, not something to pry into until she knew him better.

The restaurant where Davin pulled into the parking lot looked like little more than a white frame shack attached precariously to the side of a long pier. On top a red neon sign flashed on and off, 'Fish House', in an inelegant but direct statement of its nature. Outside the air was pungent and salty, but inside it was a *mélange* of fish and beer. Brightly lighted beer signs reflected in the polished bar. Tables with red checked cloths and dark bentwood chairs were set about in the middle of the large square room, booths around the edges. Davin led the way to a corner booth, a little more private than the rest.

'Is this the pier where your friend has his boat?' asked Susanna.

Davin nodded.

'Do I get to meet him?'

He nodded again. 'He knows the whole story,' he said, with a meaningful look at her.

'Am I being trotted by for his approval?'

'No.' There was a humorous twist to the corner of Davin's mouth, but he did not elaborate. Instead he suggested they start their dinner with a bowl of fish chowder, followed by crab legs, sourdough bread, and a salad.

'Sounds wonderful—I'm starved!' Susanna replied, realising that she had not eaten a decent meal in two days.

As soon as the waiter had taken their order and brought them two frosty mugs of beer, Davin pulled out a pad and pencil. 'I've been trying to lay out the next couple of weeks,' he said. 'At first I thought we'd go out to some fancy night spot every night for the first week, but hell, I wouldn't do that with someone I really cared for, and neither would you. We'll just come here or some equally quiet place, or go to my house . . . or yours, if I'm invited.' He looked up and she dimpled.

'Trying to find out if I can cook?' she teased. 'Of course you're invited. Any time.'

'All right, I'll come home with you tomorrow, then.'

'But I'm not working tomorrow.'

Davin frowned. 'Says who?'

'Sally gave me the day off.' Susanna grinned mischievously. 'You see, yesterday was such a rotten day and I was so tired, and I just wanted a chance to rest up. I didn't get much chance to rest today, either. But if you insist, Mr Sigmundsen, sir, I'll be there.'

'Don't bother.' Davin's sigh was resigned. 'Just have a fabulous dinner waiting for me.'

'Yes, sir.'

'And don't say "yes, sir"!' This time his glare was real and Susanna threw back her head and laughed.

'No, sir,' she answered meekly, and caught the twinkle returning to Davin's eyes.

Over their soup course Davin jotted down his plans for each night: your place, back to the Fish House, my house . . .

'Do you like Beethoven?' he asked suddenly.

'Love him,' Susanna answered a little mushily, her mouth full of soup.

Davin smiled, very pleased. 'Good. We'll keep the concert, then.' He made a few more notes. 'Next Saturday there's a *première* we'll take in, then a party afterwards at the producer's. There'll be a lot of press there. We'll announce our engagement then.'

Susanna nearly choked. 'Next Saturday already?'

'Well, that's five days away. We can't wait until the day before the wedding.'

'I guess not.' She wiped her chin. 'Do you mind if I call my parents and tell them Friday night, then? I don't want them to hear the news first on the television or something.'

'Of course. Do you think they'll want to come for the wedding?' David looked up again and then nodded after seeing her disgusted expression. 'Of course they will. I'll see that we have a room ready for them, send them their plane tickets.' He scribbled some more.

'They can afford their own tickets,' said Susanna, a little coldly.

Sensing the chill, Davin added, 'I feel it's only fair I do it when I'm stealing their daughter at such short notice.' His eyebrows were raised questioningly, but she felt it would be useless to argue. Besides, it would make a real dent in her parents' budget, while Davin would not even notice it.

'That's all right,' she said. 'They won't mind.'

'Good.' The paper and pencil were put away when the steaming platter of crab legs was brought, and both of them were busily cracking open the shells and pulling out the long, delicious chunks of sweet meat. Finally, after devouring five of the huge legs, a large slice of sourdough bread, and a large part of her salad, Susanna sat back.

'I'm full up,' she breathed happily. 'That was the best dinner I've had in ages.'

Davin smiled approvingly. 'Thank God you don't nibble at your food like a spastic rabbit,' he commented. 'I detest going to dinner with those scrawny, eternally dieting females.'

'Well, I couldn't eat like this every night or I'd soon be as big as a house,' Susanna laughed, 'but I like food too much to diet all the time. Just so I don't outgrow my clothes.'

'Mmmm, that reminds me. You're to take anything you want from the store—anything. It will be yours to keep.'

'Oh, I couldn't!' cried Susanna, thinking of the fabulous clothes and jewels that had just been laid before her, almost as if it were only a child's Christmas.

'Yes, you *could*.' Davin's deep voice was commanding. 'And don't you dare say "yes sir",' he added as she opened her mouth.

'Yes, Davin,' she said instead. 'And thank you.'

Davin reviewed his orderly plans: tomorrow, Susanna's for dinner: Wednesday, his house, meet Grandmother Sigmundsen; Thursday, concert; Friday, dinner out, call Susanna's family; Saturday, the premiere; Sunday, picnic on the beach; Monday, dinner out, place to be decided; etc. Susanna felt like troops being given their marching orders.

'Let's go and meet Hank,' Davin said finally, putting away his notes and rising.

'Forward march!' Susanna said brightly.

He looked unhappy. 'I'm sorry if I come off as terribly bossy. It's just that there's so much to get done in a short time.'

'I was only teasing.' It was amazing how sensitive Davin was to every nuance of her moods. Susanna took his hand and squeezed it. 'I just wish I could be more help.' She was rewarded by that gentle half-smile that she was beginning to know meant real appreciation on Davin's part.

She took an instant liking to Hank Trimble, who welcomed them on to the deck of his fishing trawler with as much quiet dignity as a king receiving guests at his castle. He was wiry and weatherbeaten, with black hair and piercingly direct blue eyes, eyes which mirrored the directness of his speech, Susanna found, as he ushered them below and brought out some Mexican beer.

'You're looking very calm and collected for someone who's taking on this big character for a husband,' he commented as he handed her a bottle.

'I told you she was a fine actress,' Davin put in before she could reply.

'Not that good,' Susanna laughed. 'Maybe I'm just relieved. I thought Davin was going to fire me.'

'You *what*?' Davin's eyebrows rose in surprise.

She explained about her fears, ending with a demonstration of the face she had made behind her customers' backs which left Hank roaring with laughter.

'You've picked a winner there, Davin old pal,' he said. 'You sure it's only going to be for a year?'

It was a question that Davin did not answer. He only smiled and changed the subject, enquiring after Hank's fishing fortunes.

As they were leaving, after an interval of congenial conversation, Susanna said, 'Could we come out with you some time, Hank? I'd really like to. If women are allowed, that is.' She saw the two men exchange a meaningful look over her head, the corner of Davin's mouth curving in a smile.

'Any time,' grinned Hank. 'Any time at all.'

Davin was whistling softly to himself as they walked back to the car.

'Did I pass the test?' asked Susanna.

'And then some,' he commented a little dryly as he helped her into the car.

Instead of heading home, Davin drove to a spot where they could walk along the beach. Susanna took off her sandals, running through the soft sand and down to the cool firm sand where the foam curled up and tickled her toes before retreating to its mother wave. Davin too took off his shoes and they both turned up their jeans, walking along hand in hand through the shallow edge of the water, then pausing to sit on some rocks that jutted to the water's edge. It was Susanna who broke the spell of silence that had overtaken them. She rubbed her sand-encrusted foot against Davin's long and bony one.

'My goodness, you do have big feet,' she said teasingly, smiling up at Davin.

He smiled, looking down for a moment at their touching toes and then rubbing against hers, the sand between them showering off until there was nothing but the warmth of bare skin on bare skin. The arm which he had tucked around her pulled her closer, his other hand caressed her cheek, and pushed back her hair as his mouth closed over hers slowly, almost tentatively. And then it was as if some connection had been made, from head to toe, and their bodies were straining together. His hand tugged her blouse free and felt along her rib cage, coming up to cup her breast, stroking softly as her nipples hardened in response. She felt as if she were sinking into a sweet, delicious fog from which she never wanted to escape. It was the sound of laughter from a distance down the shore that brought her back to reality, made her gently push herself free.

'This is still only our first date,' she reminded Davin huskily, 'and I'm still the girl from Iowa, remember? I must say you're getting into your part very well.' She tucked her shirt in again and stared at him reprovingly.

'You *are* very beautiful,' he said soberly. 'Don't worry, I can control myself.'

'You may have to control both of us,' Susanna thought to herself grimly. There was something about the warm, solid, masculine feel of Davin's body that set off sensations in her own that had been long suppressed, almost forgotten. It felt so good, so right, to be close to him. 'Watch out!' she warned herself, shivering a little as Davin's arm encircled her once again as they started to walk back towards the car. It would not do to get too used to that pleasant closeness.

'Cold?' Davin asked, feeling her shiver.

'No.' Susanna sighed to herself. Perhaps she might as well admit to a strong physical attraction to Davin. It was there. She could not very well tell him not to touch her, because it would be impossible to carry off their illusion of a passionate romance if he stood three feet away from her all the time. And if they behaved entirely differently when they were alone they would surely slip up in public. Probably, she thought hopefully, the physical part would fade as they grew better acquainted. That often happened.

CHAPTER THREE

IT was after ten the next morning when the persistent sound of knocking on her door woke Susanna. She smiled to herself and stretched drowsily, reaching for her robe. She had dreamed the night away in a delicious fantasy of snuggling close to Davin, and even though it had only been her pillow that she clutched, it had been most pleasant. With a still dreamy expression on her face she opened the door to Maria.

Maria's face broke into a wide smile as she entered the apartment and stood looking at her friend. 'Behold, a lady in love,' she chuckled softly. 'I knew when you got home so late that you did not spend all that time talking business!'

Susanna blinked, her mind beginning to work. 'Well . . .' she said slowly, 'we did have a lovely evening. We ended up walking along the shore.' She dimpled at the remembrance of Davin's kiss there, and at the one he had given her when he brought her in, less passionate but still enough to set her heart to tripping. 'He's coming to dinner tonight,' she added as she set her coffee pot to working and glanced around the little kitchen. 'I wonder what I should have?'

'If he's as smitten as you are it won't make much difference,' Maria said sagely.

'Now don't you go rushing things,' Susanna scolded. 'Davin's been out with dozens of girls more glamorous and exciting than I am. I hardly imagine I bowled him over in one evening. I think I'd better come up with a

pretty special dinner. Bohemian chicken is my forte. Do
you think he'd like that?'

'Oh, yes! That's delicious. So different, too.'

'Then I'll make that, and mashed potatoes and gravy
and peas with pearl onions and a salad.' She paused
thoughtfully. 'I'll make some brownies first off, and get
some ice cream to go with them.'

Susanna scurried around frantically the rest of the
day, shopping, baking, cooking. The first batch of
brownies was not up to standard, and she discarded
them and began again, a desperate eye on the clock.
Reminders to herself that she had no need to be nervous
did nothing to alter the situation. She barely had time to
slip into a cool, light blue sleeveless dress and white
high-heeled sandals and anxiously make one last check
on the progress of her dinner before Davin knocked on
the door. His face, when she opened the door, did
nothing to relieve her anxiety. He looked as coolly
distant as when he was inspecting one of the displays at
the store.

'Come in,' invited Susanna, smiling politely, willing
her face not to sag in disappointment at Davin's rever-
sion to his usual restraint.

'Thank you.' He stepped inside and handed her a
bottle of wine. 'I hope this is satisfactory.'

Susanna barely glanced at the label, feeling a distinct
chill in Davin's voice. 'It's fine,' she said thinly. 'Would
you like a drink before dinner?'

'Yes, I could use a Martini.' Davin followed her into
the living room and sat down stiffly. He was dressed in a
dark grey three-piece suit, the kind Susanna had often
seen him wear around the store. With it had returned his
tightly disciplined personality.

Silently wishing she had told him to wear jeans,

Susanna mixed Davin's Martini.

'Bad day at the store?' she asked as she handed it to him.

'No worse than usual,' was the cryptic reply.

Any hopes that she had that a couple of drinks might get him to relax were soon dashed. During dinner he discussed local politics, progress on the film Susanna had been in, and the relative merits of California wines. There was a strange blankness to his expression, as if it were a mask, and she wondered if others saw this, or only saw a restrained, cultured gentleman.

After dinner, Davin sat on the couch drinking his coffee. Susanna put a Brahms symphony on the stereo and came to sit beside him, hoping that the warmth and passion of Brahms might get him to unbend. He immediately launched into a description of his grandmother, whom he called Olga. She was, Susanna gathered, a very proper and strait-laced old lady, who would want to see her great-grandson brought up strictly and to be a proper little gentleman. Davin went over his plans for Bobby, how he hoped he would be a good athlete as well as an excellent student, perhaps becoming a doctor or lawyer when he was grown up. Susanna wondered frantically where the Davin she had been out with the previous night had gone. Had that just been an act, the jokes, the laughter, the friendly give and take? She stared at Davin, stifling a yawn. No, she decided, this was the phoney one. But why?

'Tired?' he asked.

'No.' She looked at her watch. 'It's early. It's rather warm in here.' Suddenly an idea came to her. 'Take off your coat,' she coaxed, standing up and and holding out her hand.

For a moment Davin looked as if he might refuse, but

instead he leaned forward and shrugged it off.

'Your waistcoat, too,' Susanna ordered sweetly, taking it from him as he complied, looking rather puzzled. She knelt down on the couch beside him, looking him over thoughtfully. His tie was still fastened tightly, his white shirt impeccable. Susanna leaned over and undid the tie and tossed it across the room, then unbuttoned several buttons of his shirt, aware that he was sitting very still, his face a careful blank.

'There,' she said, pushing his shirt front open. 'Now you look almost human.' She put on her most passionately adoring look and leaned forward, her face close to his. 'What do you think,' she murmured breathlessly, 'about the price of kites?'

He stared back at her, his lips twitching and his eyes beginning to lose their glassy impersonality. 'Too high?' he ventured.

'Much too high,' Susanna answered in sultry tones. 'What do you think about the price of elevators?'

'Going up?' He was grinning now.

'Nooo,' she said with a sensual moan. 'Going down.' She reached up and stroked his forehead. 'Have you heard about the diaper market?'

Davin started chuckling helplessly. 'I suppose it's hit bottom?'

'Right!' She clapped her hands and sat back down, laughing with him. 'Welcome back. Who was that other fellow that was here? I didn't like him very well.'

He looked at her warily. 'You're much too astute. He was the fellow who keeps the Davin you seem to prefer in line.'

'You have trouble with this one?'

He nodded. 'I used to.' He seemed to be looking back to another time, lines of pain drawing his eyes almost shut. 'He acted before he thought, seldom thought about tomorrow, was terribly naïve . . .'

'Got badly hurt?' Susanna questioned softly.

'That too,' he admitted, his eyes seeking hers. 'I'm not about to let that happen again.'

He was warning her, Susanna realised, that he would not let her get too close, their friendly marriage ripen into a real one. She sighed. 'I just want to be friends with this one. I really can't see putting up with that stuffy bloke, even for a year. Surely you don't act that way around Hank?'

'He wouldn't let me,' Davin answered with a grin, 'any more than you will, I'm afraid. That's what worries me.'

'Afraid of opening Pandora's box?'

'Something like that.'

She looked at him seriously. 'Want to fire me?'

'No.' He shook his head slowly, his eyes still worried but clear and sea-green again. 'I probably should, but no. Want to quit?'

'No.'

'Then don't say I didn't warn you. Two of us who like to live dangerously in the same house might present a problem.'

'Me?' Susanna's forehead puckered into a quizzical frown. 'I never thought of myself that way.' She reviewed her life quickly, including her recent acquisition of a decidedly off-beat job. 'I guess there's some truth in it,' she admitted, 'but I'm not afraid of it.'

'Maybe that's because you've never really been hurt. Let's hope it stays that way.'

Susanna studied the handsome face, no longer like chiselled stone but warmly appealing, the mouth that could be so stern now curved in sensuous lines, the velvety depths of his eyes beckoning like some forbidden lagoon. 'That's a chance I'll have to take,' she answered with a smile.

'What's this with you and Davin Sigmundsen?' demanded Sally the moment she saw Susanna in the morning. 'He told me to outfit you in something terrific for the *première* on Saturday. Are you going with him?'

'Mmm-hmm,' Susanna replied with a mysterious little smile, that had the desired effect of sending Sally into a persistent torrent of questions, all of which Susanna evaded with demure charm, except for purposely letting slip the fact that she was also going to the symphony concert with Davin the following evening. Sally would doubtless disseminate this information far and wide, starting the inevitable rumour process in motion.

Susanna only saw Davin once during the day, as she was picking out some accessories to complement an outfit she was to model for some society women that afternoon.

'Good morning, Miss Blair,' he said with a formal little nod.

Susanna raised her eyebrows and smiled faintly. 'It's afternoon, sir,' she replied. She picked up the shoes, scarf and handbag she had chosen and, returning his formal nod, turned and walked away. In one of the mirrored pillars she could see Davin's reflection as he looked after her, valiantly trying to keep from smiling. What a strange and fascinating man he was! It was probably not wise for her to try to strip away his hard-won dignity when he was at the store, for he seemed to feel he needed it in order to function properly in the world of business, Susanna mused as she helped Sally arrange the sequence for the afternoon's brief showing.

But it was such a temptation, the reward of his face changing from sombre to sunlit so great, that it was almost irresistible. She had spent much of the night debating the wisdom of her choice, returning again and again to her previous decision, although she knew full well it was not based on any rational thought. It was a chance she had to take. At least she would not be around the store much longer to pester him, she thought with a sigh.

'Fallen for him like a ton, haven't you?' Sally commented smugly. 'Somehow I wouldn't have thought him your type, with all that icy elegance. Or does he warm up when you get to know him?'

'He's very charming,' Susanna replied coolly. No need for everyone in the world to know there was a Davin Sigmundsen who walked barefoot in the sand in the moonlight or cracked up over silly jokes. Oh, yes, he could be warm indeed. There had been that kiss on the beach, and then the one last night. Last night he had merely taken her face between his hands as he said good night, kissing her for a long time, very gently. But somehow that kiss had meant more, the contained fire of his touch clinging to her cheeks for a long time. It had meant, Susanna thought, an acceptance of her as someone who was privileged to know the other Davin, with all his flaws, real or imagined. She put her hand to her cheek as if the touch still lingered.

'Yoo-hoo!' Sally called brightly. 'Come down from your cloud! It's time to start dressing.'

The clothes that Susanna was to model this afternoon were the epitome of understated elegance, the kind she usually adored, but something restless inside her made the job less pleasant than usual. She longed instead for something bright coloured, wildly high-fashion. It was

Davin, she realised as she put on a clinging full-length black evening gown. The clothes made her feel as if a stiff formality were closing in on her, too. Her hair swept up, a choker of diamonds around her neck, she paraded before the two women and their daughters, whose looks of carefully arranged boredom never changed.

'I think that might do,' she heard one of them drawl in a monotone.

'For two thousand plus it ought to,' Susanna thought as she smiled faintly and turned, walking away from the women to show off the deeply cut back of the dress. A movement in the curtains caught her eyes, and Davin appeared, out of sight of the women, watching her as if she were a mobile post. 'There's Mr Stuffy again,' she thought to herself. She sucked in her cheeks and gave him a look of utterly bored hauteur, wishing she dared break into her Katherine Hepburn imitation. Davin's only response was a slight raising of his eyebrows. Disgusted, Susanna finished displaying the gown and made her exit without another glance in his direction. Davin appeared in the dressing room at the same moment as she did.

'I like that dress on you, Susanna,' he said calmly. 'Wear it to the concert tomorrow.' He turned to Sally, who was staring at him open-mouthed. 'Put that aside for Miss Blair. The necklace too.'

'But what if Mrs Overstreet wants it?' Sally stammered weakly.

'Tell her it had some flaw in it we just discovered.'

Susanna looked frantically from Davin to Sally and back. What was Sally going to think of this latest extravagant gift? She was pretty sure she knew, and soon the whole town would be talking about the blonde actress Davin Sigmundsen had taken as his mistress.

'But I don't want it,' Susanna objected. 'I don't even like it! And from what I heard, Mrs Overstreet does. She'll be furious—and that's not good business.'

'I think I know how to run my store,' Davin said mildly.

'But . . .'

'Don't be argumentative, Susanna.' He looked at his watch. 'It's getting late. Meet me in my office in half an hour.' With that he turned on his heel and left, Susanna glaring after his departing back.

'He hasn't even *seen* argumentative yet,' she muttered, her jaw set defiantly. She turned to Sally with a frown. 'This isn't what it looks like,' she said firmly. 'We're just . . . friends.'

Sally raised her eyebrows and smiled knowingly. 'Whatever it is, it's mighty interesting!'

Susanna had brought her own outfit with her to wear to Davin's home to meet his grandmother—a slim dress and jacket of natural raw silk, bone-coloured shoes and bag, a discreet turquoise pendant and earrings, the total impression was tastefully elegant. 'Just the right thing to meet a proper lady,' Susanna thought as she fastened her earrings. It promised to be a very proper evening indeed. She did want to make a good impression on Davin's grandmother, but tomorrow night was another question entirely. With a determined step she marched towards Davin's office. His secretary was already gone, his door open, and he was still studying some papers on his desk as Susanna entered with a light tap on the door to let him know she was there. He looked up.

'You look very nice,' he said as his eyes flicked up and down her body. 'Sit down. I'll be with you in a minute.'

She perched on the edge of a chair, watching as

Davin's head bent over the papers, and he occasionally made swift slashing movements with a pen across the pages. In a few minutes he completed his task, tucked the papers into his briefcase, and stood up.

'Ready?' he said, taking her arm and propelling her out of the door.

Susanna did not answer. Of course she was ready, she thought grimly, but not for all this bossing around.

'I do *not* want to wear that black dress tomorrow,' she said as they walked towards the small parking lot where the staff parked.

'But you look very lovely in it. You rather remind me of an Egyptian princess.'

'With blonde hair?' Susanna snorted. 'Hardly likely. Besides, what if Mrs Overstreet is at the concert? She'll know who I am and where the dress came from, and there's just one conclusion she'll draw. And I don't like it.'

Davin looked at her coolly. 'So? She'll soon find out differently.'

'Davin, please! Why are you being so stubborn? I don't want that dress. I have one at home that's every bit as suitable that I like much better.'

'Are you sure it's not you that's being stubborn?'

She stopped walking and glared up at Davin, who looked back at her from behind his almost expression-less mask. 'Damn you!' she snapped. 'I don't care who's being stubborn. I will not wear that dress, and I will not be pushed around like some kind of robot. And don't think you can retreat into that iron-clad shell of yours and get away with it. Others may jump to when you snap your fingers, but I won't.'

'All right,' Davin shrugged, 'have it your way.' He turned and walked towards the one remaining car in the lot and Susanna followed, exasperated that she had not got even a small rise out of him. It was almost as if he was dead when he put on his protective shell. He stopped and opened the car door for her, and it was only then that she really saw the car. It was a bright red Ferrari.

'Davin!' she almost shrieked. 'What have you done? You got the . . . why did you? I mean, for heaven's sake, you can't just . . .' She stopped babbling and stared up at his impassive countenance.

'Actually,' he said, still in a calm voice, 'I thought it might give the right impression. After all, if I'm about to abandon bachelorhood after thirty-five years something must have knocked all the sense out of me.'

'Oh, I see,' Susanna said acidly. 'It's just part of the props, just stage dressing. How clever of you! Well, I hope the car fools somebody. That face of yours certainly won't.' She started to get into the car, but Davin's hand on her arm pulled her back and turned her to face him as he stood grinning down at her, his shoulders shaking with silent laughter.

'It fooled you pretty well,' he chuckled, his eyes sparkling mischievously. 'And I really got the car because I thought you would enjoy it. Do you mind?'

'Mind?' Susanna shook her head in amazement. 'Of course not. It's just that . . . oh, never mind.' She smiled happily, more at the sudden transformation in Davin than at the car.

'Good. And you certainly needn't wear that dress tomorrow. You look so lovely in it that I never thought about the impression it might create. I wouldn't want you to be embarrassed.' He bent swiftly and kissed her smiling lips. 'Come on, we'd better get going. Olga doesn't like to be kept waiting.'

CHAPTER FOUR

'How shall I behave in front of your grandmother?' Susanna asked as they drove along Sunset Boulevard towards Bel Air. 'Shall I be cool and sophisticated, sweet and adoring, or just pick on you like I usually do?'

Davin chuckled. 'You mean which is most likely to convince Olga that this might be a serious affair?'

'Yes. After all, she must know you pretty well.'

'You can say that again,' he said vehemently. He slowed the powerful car so as not to arrive at his home too soon. 'Olga may be almost eighty, but she's extremely sharp. She's been around the movie industry almost since its beginning, and if anyone can tell an act from the real thing it's her. Not only that, but I'm sure she knows only too well what I think of the bored sophisticate or the simpering ingénue. I think it will be best if you just be your usual . . . er . . . forthright self. Just try not to look as if you hate me.'

'Well, I don't, so that's no problem,' Susanna said with a quick smile.

'I was wondering for a little while back there,' Davin replied, but his relaxed manner assured her that he was not really worried.

They turned into a street lined with elegant houses, then on to another where the homes were so elegant that they were obscured from view by what seemed like miles of high walls and fences. Davin slowed near a gap in one of the walls and turned in between iron gates that opened at a touch of a button on his dashboard.

'Good heavens!' Susanna exclaimed. 'I've never been in a place like this before.' She had visions of a huge mausoleum of a house, and throngs of liveried servants. The drive wound between tall old live oak trees set in a beautifully manicured lawn. Then, suddenly, the house came into view, curled against a hillside like a lazy cat, a sprawling expanse of redwood and stone and glass. The house seemed to stretch for hundreds of feet, curving away from the entrance portico on both sides and rising slightly on one side as it attempted to climb a small hill. 'Oh! This is lovely,' she exclaimed as her eyes swept from one end to the other. 'I expected something more traditional, probably older.'

'There was a house like that here not too many years ago,' Davin told her with a smile. 'Not too long after Grandfather Sigmundsen died there was a serious fire, and rather than rebuild the old place, Olga and I decided to just start over. She said the old house was full of too many memories, too much a relic of the past.'

'How remarkable,' Susanna said in surprise. 'Most older people like to cling to the past.'

'Olga is remarkable,' said Davin, taking her arm and leading her towards the door. 'I think you're going to like each other.'

The door was opened by a tall, elderly man in a plain dark suit.

'This is Jarl, Susanna,' Davin introduced her. 'Jarl came here from Minnesota not long after Olga did, and he's been with the family as chauffeur and chief assistant on everything ever since.'

'How do you do, Jarl,' Susanna smiled, holding out her hand.

'I'm very pleased to meet you,' the elderly gentleman said in a slightly accented voice, gripping her hand firmly. He looked at Davin. 'Your grandmother is not quite ready. She will join you in about fifteen minutes.'

'Thank you, Jarl. That will give me time to show Susanna around a little.'

Jarl smiled pleasantly and nodded, then silently turned and walked towards the back of the house, past the huge atrium which sprang up in the middle of the parqueted entry foyer, itself large enough, Susanna thought, for a dance hall. Far beyond she could see a wall of glass and the shimmering reflections of sunshine on water, a pool of some kind, she imagined. Davin took her arm and led her to the left, down several steps into the expansive living room with its vaulted ceiling and immense stone fireplace. The carpet was cream-coloured, the furniture in shades of beige and brown, but everywhere there were splashes of colour: in cushions and throw-overs, vases and flowers. On one white-painted wall was a large painting of a mother and child in a meadow blossoming with flowers. Susanna headed straight for it, drawn by its vivid beauty. She had no doubt whose signature would be in the corner: D. Sigmundsen.

'Oooh!' she breathed, staring entranced at the passionate evocation of mother love and spring and sunshine. She looked at Davin, who was watching her very soberly. 'Do you still paint?'

'No.' His mouth tightened as he said it.

'Why on earth not? I'm no expert, but I think you have remarkable talent.'

Davin shrugged, his eyes distant. 'I haven't the time to waste.' He gestured to the door at the end of the room which opened on to a long hallway. 'That leads to Olga's rooms. She has her own little suite, so she can have her privacy when she wants it.' He took Susanna's elbow in his large hand. 'I want to show you the other wing. The formal dining room is back there.' He indicated an arched doorway on one side of the fireplace. 'You'll see that shortly.'

They crossed the foyer again and entered another hallway which ran along the front of the house. The first rooms Davin showed her were the guest suite, a comfortable, colourful bedroom, sitting room and bath. The hallway rose two steps and Davin threw open another door. 'These will be our rooms,' he said softly.

Susanna stepped into the large bedroom and looked about her. Again, the colours were softly muted, shades of green and turquoise used as accent colours against the creamy carpet and white walls. One wall was almost entirely swathed in airy draperies. There were two beds, both larger than an ordinary double bed, with quilted spreads in a soft turquoise accented with silver threads.

'We're going to sleep in the same room?' she asked, keeping her voice low also.

Davin nodded, looking at her a little anxiously. 'This house doesn't lend itself to any other arrangement, except something that would arouse a lot of suspicion. There's only one other bedroom, down past my study, and that will be Bobby's.'

'Oh.' Susanna's brow puckered into a frown. Two people who liked to live dangerously sleeping in the same room every night might prove to be a problem.

'Do you object?' Davin's face was so boyishly worried that she smiled comfortingly.

'I guess we can make it work out. Just put on your stuffy Mr Store Owner face and *I* won't be tempted, and I expect I can be bitchy enough to keep you in your place if necessary.'

Davin chuckled at that. 'Then I'll have to be good. I can't say I've seen you being "bitchy" yet, but I definitely wouldn't look forward to it.'

'I thought that was what I was this afternoon,' Susanna said with a coy look from under her eyelashes.

'Not at all. You had a perfectly legitimate complaint,' Davin answered. 'Bitchy is when you complain for no reason.' He grinned. 'Come on and see Sigmundsen's folly.' He led her across the room and flung open the door to the most exotic bathroom complex she had ever seen. There was a mammoth sunken marble tub with gold fittings, a wall of glass opening on to a tiny private patio, and beyond, a dressing room with two tremendous walk-in closets, a mirrored sitting room, and even a built-in bar and tiny kitchenette. 'Olga says I was over-compensating for the fact that my fishing cabin has no inside plumbing,' he said as Susanna stared in open-mouthed awe.

'This is unreal,' she whispered. 'This really makes me feel like Cinderella! I can't even imagine getting used to such luxury.'

Davin smiled gently. 'See that girl over there?' He pointed to Susanna's reflection in the long mirrors. 'She looks to me like she belongs here.'

Susanna looked at her own reflection, elegant in her trim suit, her upswept hair shining in a golden halo as the light caught the soft waves of her crown. It was true, she did not look out of place, but it was only her temporary surroundings, she reminded herself. 'If the folks back in Iowa could see me now!' she said with a little laugh, trying to bring herself back to earth. She was only there for a moment, for Davin quickly folded her into his arms and kissed her, his lips warm and possessive, his arms tightening around her as she responded eagerly. In a few seconds he let her go and drew back, looking down at her with a bemused smile.

'You're an amazing girl, Susanna,' he said slowly. 'I know I'm asking a lot of you, but I promise you won't regret it.'

As Susanna's heartbeat gradually slowed she looked into the deep sea-green eyes, so intense beneath their fringe of dark lashes.

'One can't always be sure of such things,' she said thoughtfully, her tingling senses telling her in no uncertain terms that there was but one regret she had at the moment. 'But I'll do my best to see that you have no regrets either.'

'I know that,' said Davin, his deep voice husky. He took a deep breath. 'I expect it's time to meet Olga.'

Formidable was the one word Susanna would have chosen to describe Olga Sigmundsen. She was almost six feet tall, slender and erect, with the prominent cheekbones and slightly slanted eyes of a true Scandinavian. Her hair was silver, her eyes a bright, piercing blue. She wore a black dress that Susanna recognised must be vintage Chanel, still as trimly stylish as the day it was made. She held out her hand and inclined her head graciously as Davin introduced Susanna to her.

'How do you do, Susanna? Davin tells me you're from Iowa. I spent my childhood in Minnesota, and I still miss the snow in the winter.' She went on reminiscing and comparing notes with Susanna over cocktails, then led the way into the dining room when Jarl announced that dinner was served.

The dining room was another surprise for Susanna, for instead of being stiffly formal, the furniture was casual, the table one that could pull out to seat a dozen or more or be folded back into a cabinet when the glass wall that opened out on to the flagstone terrace and the swimming pool was pushed back. Susanna realised that the curtained wall in the master bedroom must hide another entrance to the pool deck. In the dusk, lanterns illuminated the outside scene and the gardens beyond the pool like a set from some lavish movie. Soft music came from hidden speakers. Entranced, she stared out the window until Davin cleared his throat and she jerked her head towards him, surprised that the real world was still present.

'I was waiting for Ginger Rogers and Fred Astaire to come dancing by,' she said with a smile, helping herself from the dish of potatoes that Jarl was holding out for her. 'Thank you,' she said, and received a warm smile from that elderly gentleman, as well as an approving look from Olga, who had been watching her intently.

Susanna's remark about Astaire and Rogers sparked a lively discussion of the movies, past and present, with Olga furnishing many anecdotes about people she had known well but who to Susanna were more the stuff of legends. As the dinner neared its conclusion, the topic turned to pet peeves, and Susanna put forward hers.

'Nothing annoys me more than sloppiness in little details,' she confessed.

'That's one area where Cyril and you agree,' said Davin with a grin. 'His films are practically faultless.'

'Not quite,' Susanna said dryly. 'I had to correct an error in *Murder for Fun* myself. Actually it was a script error. The gun used by the long-distance sniper was called a twenty-two when actually it was a twenty-two two-fifty. I grew up around guns and hunters,' she explained to Olga, who had an amused smile on her face.

'You seem to have had to straighten Cyril out quite a

bit,' Olga commented with a meaningful lift of her eyebrows.

Susanna stopped with her fork half way to her mouth and glared at Davin. 'Davin, you didn't have to . . .' she began, but he interrupted.

'No, I didn't have to. Olga was present when Cyril came that night, and she saw him before I dragged him off to the study. Naturally, I had to explain later what had happened to him.'

'Naturally,' Susanna agreed with a resigned sigh. She wondered what the dignified lady sitting across from her thought of a young woman who allowed herself to get in a position where such violent measures were necessary.

Shortly after dessert was served, Jarl appeared to tell Davin that he had a telephone call, and Davin excused himself, leaving the two women alone.

'Thank goodness,' Olga sighed as soon as he had left the room. 'He can be terribly hard to get rid of.' She leaned forward, her bright eyes studying Susanna with unusual intensity.

Susanna returned her gaze, wondering what kind of cross-examination Olga had been waiting to give her, hoping that she could stay on her toes enough to give satisfactory answers. She was quite unprepared for Olga's opening statement.

'You really have my grandson in a spin, Susanna,' the old woman said, her features changing from rather severe to warm, her eyes to a friendly sparkle, even as Davin's could do. 'I haven't had such a pleasant dinner with him in years. He's been more inclined to imitate something from the wax museum.'

Suppressing an urge to giggle, Susanna smiled im-pishly. 'He can be rather that way, can't he? But I thought that was just a front he used in public. Surely he hasn't been that way at home all the time?' She sobered as Olga pursed her lips and nodded sadly.

'Most of the time. It's been like pulling teeth to get a laugh out of him. How did you do it?'

Susanna thought quickly. She had seen the veneer crack when Davin began to talk about Bobby, but she could not tell Olga that. Then there was the episode of the blue jeans, but that might sound a little strange. 'I just pick on him a lot, I guess,' she said finally with a little smile.

Olga cocked a knowing eyebrow. 'I won't press you for the details,' she said with a sly chuckle. 'Just keep it up, whatever it is.' She leaned towards Susanna again. 'Do you find Davin attractive?'

At this blunt question Susanna almost lost her composure, forcing herself to resist the impulse to babble some silly reply. 'Yes, I do,' she answered honestly as soon as she was sure of her voice. 'I like him very much. Why do you ask?' Be forthright, Davin had said. Olga certainly was, her next statement even more so.

'Because Davin should get married. For years he's only brought young women home to dinner to show me how impossible it would be for him to marry any of them. With you, I'm quite sure, it's a different story altogether.'

'Oh.' Susanna could think of no reply to that, dropping her eyes to stare at the wine glass she was turning around and around in her fingers. Olga obviously thought she detected a profound change in her grandson, unaware that he was deceiving her. Or was he? Perhaps she really had had a good effect on Davin, independent of their plans for a contract marriage. Had he simply not chosen to drop his façade in the past, or had he been unable to? That was a puzzle Susanna could not solve at the moment. Of more concern was her own response to Olga's interest in her plans for the future with Davin. What if there had not been any talk of marriage before? How would she feel now? There was the strong physical attraction she felt, but even more pleasant was the pleasure that seeing Davin relaxed and smiling gave to her. She pictured him as she had seen him first, his eyes clouded, his expressionless mask in place, and then with his eyes sparkling with laughter or deep green with passion, his mouth warm against hers. She cared a great deal about keeping that wide, sensuous mouth curved upward in a smile, she thought, her own mouth curving into a smile as she had the thought. She looked up at Olga, who was regarding her intently.

'We'll just have to see what happens,' she said softly, knowing as she did so that she was admitting to herself for the first time that her relationship with Davin was one that she might like to see progress to something more permanent, a dangerous notion for a Cinderella wife. She looked anxiously into Olga's bright blue eyes. How much did she see? Would she now be prepared when Davin told her he was going to marry her? She quickly had her answer to that.

'I expect you'll be getting a proposal quite soon—at least if Davin has any sense. A girl as pretty as you are must have plenty of offers.'

Susanna grimaced. 'More of Cyril's type, I'm afraid. I've been too busy to build a serious relationship with anyone.'

'Well,' Olga said primly, 'you won't be hearing anything like that from Davin.'

'Oh, I didn't mean . . .' Susanna stammered, blushing.

'No, no, of course you didn't.' The old lady smiled

kindly. 'And that's the first time I've seen you flustered. I like that. I can't stand women who blush and simper. I like a girl who can keep her head.' She paused. 'I'm afraid I've been rather blunt, but Davin's unhappiness has been a great concern to me. I do so like to see him smile.'

'So do I,' Susanna agreed, just as the gentleman in question came back into the room.

'Do what?' he asked, including both women in one of those smiles they had been discussing.

'None of your business,' Olga replied tartly.

Susanna grinned. 'We've just agreed that you're the most charming man in fifty-one states.'

'I'll just bet you have,' said Davin wryly as he sat down again, but he did not question them further.

They lingered a little longer over dessert and coffee and then Olga excused herself. 'I like to take a little rest after dinner,' she told Susanna. 'I hope I'll be seeing you again soon.' As she said this she glanced sharply at Davin, who caught her meaning and smiled mischievously.

'Don't be so obvious, Olga,' he said, with a wink at Susanna.

Susanna ignored him. 'I hope so too,' she replied to Olga, raising her chin and wrinkling her nose at Davin. 'With or without your grandson.'

At this Davin rose swiftly and came around behind Susanna's chair, placing his hands on her shoulders and bending to kiss her behind the ear. 'You'll be seeing her soon,' he promised. 'With me.'

As Susanna turned her head to look up at him she could see Olga leaving the room with a pleased smile on her face, then her vision was blocked as Davin kissed her again, this time on the mouth.

He took her on a tour of the lighted part of the grounds, pointing out the tennis court and the greenhouse. Then he led her into his study, which also opened on to the pool. It was a comfortable, book-lined room, with a huge clutter desk. There was a leather sofa and there were leather armchairs facing a table on which rested a beautiful carved jade chess set. Susanna paused to examine one of the delicate pieces.

'Do you play chess?' asked Davin.

'I used to play with my brothers, but I'm not terrific,' Susanna answered.

'Let's see how good you are.' He pulled out one of the chairs for Susanna, then sat down himself after discarding his jacket and tie.

'Uh-oh, serious business,' she teasted. 'I'm not sure I'm up to your calibre of play.'

Davin got up quickly and came to remove the pins that held Susanna upswept hairdo in place. 'There,' he said as it fell in waves to her shoulders, 'now you can tear your hair or chew on it or whatever you do when you're in deep thought. Besides, I like it better down.' He sat down again, and soon they were deeply engrossed in what turned out to be quite an even game. Finally Susanna cried out,

'Check! I've got you!' She stared at Davin, wide-eyed. 'Did you let me win? I can't believe you were concentrating.'

'You are a little distracting,' Davin admitted. 'I kept watching you running your fingers through your hair.'

'I always do that,' she sighed. 'I did used to chew on it, but my mother took the flyswatter to me when I did.' She glanced at her watch. 'I'd better be getting home. We have to stop at the store and get my car.'

'I'll take you home and pick you up in the morning,'

Davin said firmly. 'It's too late for you to be out alone.'
He cheerfully ignored her protests that she frequently
had to drive at night and her mutterings about his
stubbornness and took her to her apartment, following
her inside to give her a long, delicious kiss that made her
knees weak and her heart race wildly.

'There,' he said as he drew his head back and smiled
down at her. 'We couldn't have done that in a parking
lot.'

'We could have pretended it was a drive-in movie,'
Susanna suggested, her voice breathy as she stared into
his eyes, fighting against the desire she felt to pull his
head down to hers again. She felt her cheeks grow
flushed and warm as he took her chin in his hand and
kissed her eyes, her cheeks, her lips again, then pulled
her close against his chest, resting his cheek against her
hair.

'Mmmm,' he sighed, his voice a deep groan against
her ear. 'It's going to be so good for me to have you
around,' he said softly.

In a few minutes he was gone, promising to pick her up
early the next morning. She pottered about, getting
ready for bed, her mind pushing out in various directions
like a cat trapped in a sack. It could go just so far, and
then would retreat to try another angle. Davin was
attractive, more than that, even . . . She did enjoy his
kisses, maybe too much . . . It would be better if she
kept him at arm's length when they were alone, because
. . . How did he really feel about her? Good for him . . .
Was the way he made her feel good for her? Just how did
he make her feel? . . . Olga seemed to like her . . . Her
parents would like Davin . . . They would all be so
disappointed if . . . Not *if*, when . . . Maybe . . .

She flounced down on her bed and snapped off the

light. 'Try to take one day at a time, Susanna,' she warned herself. 'One at a time.'

Davin was in high good spirits the next morning as they drove towards the store.

'No one at the store will recognise you,' Susanna warned as she finally managed to stop laughing at one of his jokes. A grin and a wink was his only reply.

Sally was fairly bursting with curiosity when she came into the stock room, the lovely gown Susanna was to wear to the premiere over her arm. 'Whatever is going on around here?' she demanded. 'I've never seen Mr Sigmundsen laugh and joke before, not in the five years I've been here.' Her eyes narrowed as she looked at Susanna's not quite innocent expression. 'You're keeping something from me, aren't you?'

'Maybe,' Susanna admitted. 'You'll find out soon enough.' And none of Sally's prying could get her to say more.

She went home early to dress for the concert in her own gown of pale lilac chiffon in a simple Grecian style, hoping that Davin would like it as well as the black one she had refused to wear.

'I do like that better,' was his first comment, setting her mind at ease for what was to be a memorable evening. He was strikingly elegant in his evening clothes, the ruffled shirt that he wore only making him look more masculine, more appealing than ever. Photographers snapped their pictures, questions were asked to which they gave politely evasive answers. Their love of the passionate music of Beethoven was a shared experience, Davin drinking it in with closed eyes, their interlaced hands communicating their mutual enjoyment. Afterwards there was dancing and champagne at a private club, the thrill of dancing with someone whose musical sense matched her own, introduction, exchanged laughter and warmth. Susanna wondered how much more like a fairytale princess she could feel.

Devin fell silent on the way home—tired, Susanna surmised. At her door he kissed her only briefly, his eyes shuttered.

'Do we have to go out again tomorrow?' asked Susanna. Tomorrow she must call her parents.

'Not if you don't want to,' Davin replied quietly. 'What would you like to do?'

She shrugged, a feeling of helplessness overcoming her. Her Davin had retreated again. What had happened? 'Maybe a picnic,' she suggested. 'Early. I have to call my parents.'

'Oh, yes, all right.' He forced his mouth into a smile. 'I'll arrange something. We'll plan to leave about three.' He put his hand on the doorknob. 'Good night, Susanna,' he said in an expressionless voice, and then he was gone.

CHAPTER FIVE

TIRED as she was, Susanna slept poorly, the memory of an enchanted evening fluttering like tattered rags in her restless dreams. A foggy morning laid another weight upon her spirits. What had gone wrong? Sally perceptively kept silent, but her sideways glances told Susanna that she must look as gloomy as she felt. What of her acting the part of a woman in love? It was more than Susanna could do. How could she pretend to be bubbling with happiness when she was more miserable than she could ever recall being before? When she almost dreaded the picnic at the beach, the sailing excursion that Davin had stoically informed her was to be their afternoon's recreation?

Davin had borrowed a friend's beach house for the day, and they stowed away their supper in the refrigerator and changed into swimsuits for an hour or two of sailing. In brief navy blue swim trunks, Davin's body was breathtaking, and Susanna felt a deep longing at the sight of him added to the ache in her heart. He was still quiet, withdrawn, excessively polite.

'That's very attractive, he said of Susanna's one-piece turquoise blue suit, but she felt he would have shown no more enthusiasm if she had appeared stark naked.

The boat was small, just comfortable for two. Davin handled it expertly, warning Susanna carefully when she needed to switch sides or duck as the boom swung around. Nothing she could say, no sally she could make, could penetrate his mask, and soon Susanna too fell silent, her thoughts veering from the call she must make that evening to the strange man with whom that call was so concerned. Could she go through with it? She stared out across the water, weighing her conflicting emotions. Now, she felt, if it were just for the money, for an adventure, she could not. If she could scrape away that inner ache and find beneath it some anger, some dislike, for Davin, she could not. But those feelings were not there, no matter how hard she tried to find them. Only a deep sadness, and a stubborn determination to release once again the smiling, happy man of only a short day before. What caused these strange shifts in his mood? She longed to cry out, 'Tell me what's wrong!' but knew instinctively that that approach would be fruitless. Studying his profile, the down-turned corners of his mouth and the tense lines etched about his eyes as he squinted against the glare, she knew only that she would have to gain his trust completely before she would ever find out what terrible hurt had made him distrust his own happiness so deeply.

The little boat scudded merrily along with its two silent passengers, Davin with one hand on the tiller, the other loosely controlling the sail, his eyes fixed blankly in the distance. He seemed not to know that Susanna was staring at him, drinking in the beauty of his broad bare shoulders, the tangle of dark red hair on his chest and his muscular thighs. Tall as he was, his proportions were perfect, and Susanna wished for the talent of a Michelangelo to capture his form in sculpture. She sighed, and Davin turned to look at her, his eyes tortured.

'Susanna,' he began in a low voice, 'are you sure . . . Susanna!' The last was a loud cry that she only dimly heard, for in his turning Davin had inadvertently let the boat turn, and the wind whipped the boom sharply across, catching her on the back of the head and throwing her to the bottom of the boat, as everything went briefly dark.

Quickly the world became only foggy again, and she heard the sail flapping loose, felt Davin pull her carefully into his arms, his hands feeling her head gently, heard him saying her name over and over as she felt his lips moving over her face, dropping kisses wherever they touched. Her eyes fluttered open.

'Hello,' she said huskily, her eyes meeting the passionate sea-green eyes she had longed to see, now dark with worry. She smiled. 'I'm all right. Just a bump on the head.'

'Thank God,' muttered Davin, his lips finding hers in a kiss that was salty with tears of relief. His hands explored her body, carefully at first as if he still feared that she was broken, then with increasing intimacy, caressing her, pushing aside her shoulder straps, until she was bare to the waist and his face was buried against her breasts. Trembling with ecstasy, Susanna held his head against her there, rubbing her cheek against his hair, drinking in the feel of his warm body mingled with the heat of the sun like two kinds of sunshine joining to light the corners of her heart. Gentle lips teased the hardened nipples and she groaned softly as desire surged through her.

'Oh, Davin!'

At the sound of his name, Davin drew his head back and looked up, a slumbrous warmth in his eyes. 'Don't ever scare me like that again,' he warned, as with his hands he moulded her swimsuit back over her breasts.

'I had to do something to get your attention,' she said,

capturing his hands to hold them against her in their caress.

'Next time,' he said as he rose to his knees and kissed her again, 'hit *me* over the head instead.'

The rest of the voyage Susanna spent nestled in Davin's arms, on a boat that might as well have been in the clouds, so buoyant did she feel at having her light-hearted companion back again. It was not until they were back at her apartment and the time approached to call her parents that Susanna's nerves tightened almost unbearably. She had never lied to them about any major thing, and it tore at her heart to do so now. If only she could tell them about Bobby . . . but that was impossible. With trembling fingers she punched out the familiar number, Davin's comforting arms about her shoulders. At the sound of her mother's voice she almost panicked, but she glanced at him, watching her so quietly, his eyes soft with understanding, and her courage returned.

'Mom,' she said breathlessly, 'I have some fantastic news.'

After that the conversation went amazingly well, everyone joining in, plans being made. Davin charmed the Blairs as well from two thousand miles away as most people could in person. It was with happy excitement that the goodbyes were said, but the moment she had hung up the phone, Susanna collapsed into Davin's arms.

'I'm glad I won't have to do that again,' she said huskily, and he gathered her close, gently massaging the knots from her neck and shoulders.

'I'm not sure I deserve what you're doing for me.' His voice grated with unhappiness, and Susanna quickly sat back and looked into his troubled face, her own anxiety forgotten.

'I think you do or I wouldn't be doing it,' she said firmly. 'Besides,' she added as Davin still looked doubtful, 'I'm not just noble and self-sacrificing. I do want to help you . . . and Bobby, but I also expect to have a wonderful time. I can just imagine telling my grandchildren about the exciting year when their crazy grandmother was married to Davin Sigmundsen!'

Davin's mouth curved into a smile. 'Maybe,' he said softly.

In the morning, Davin called her into his office and presented her with a large but simple marquise diamond ring. He seemed nervous as he slid it on to her finger, his body tense as he embraced her tightly.

'Worried about telling Olga?' Susanna questioned.

'No,' Davin replied. 'She'll be very pleased.'

She put his nervousness down to the fact that the thought of going through even a sham wedding was unnerving for a man who had been a bachelor for thirty-five years. By the time they reached his home, his calm had returned, and he was able to laugh heartily when Olga Sigmundsen responded to their announcement with a sniff.

'I suppose saying it's about time is a little trite,' she said acidly, 'but it's certainly appropriate. Come here, Susanna.' Susanna obediently went to the old woman's side and bent close to receive a kiss on the cheek. 'Take good care of him,' she ordered, 'and don't let him boss you around too much.'

'Davin—bossy?' she teased, and the two women laughed together while Davin looked sheepish.

The old family limousine, which was still kept for Olga, was brought out for the trip to the premiere, and as Susanna sat in the extravagant elegance of its interior, with Davin beside her and Jarl at the wheel, she could not help but giggle. 'Here I am in jewels and furs,' she answered Davin's questioning look, 'on my way to the ball. What I really want to know is, how did you make this limousine out of a pumpkin? I thought a carriage pulled by six prancing horses was standard.'

'Modern technology,' Davin replied with a wink. 'Nervous?'

'Not a bit.' And it was true, Susanna felt no qualms about facing the press or her friends at the party, even less about meeting the dignitaries she knew would be present. The hard part was over. She knew she looked her best, the square-necked romantic gown with its filmy sleeves and billowing skirt, bands of seed pearl embroidery around the waist, neckline and cuffs, making her feel as well as look like a fairytale princess. Her hair was worn down, at Davin's command.

'Every director in Hollywood will want you when they see you like that,' he told her. 'And then I'm going to whisk you away, out of their reach. But when it comes time to resume your career, they'll remember.'

'Sort of like playing hard to get?'

'Exactly.'

It was fun to be at the premiere with Davin. The best seats, deferential attention. Susanna wondered how long it would have taken to get there on her own. She and Davin sat close, their hands interlocked, exchanging frequent comments on the film in which Susanna found numerous flaws.

'I may have to hire you as a director,' Davin whispered in her ear. 'I think Cyril's losing his touch.'

'Which one?' Susanna asked dryly, and he grinned and squeezed her hand.

The party was at a palatial mansion, a relic of the

Twenties with terraced gardens, splashing fountains, and multicoloured floodlights playing on the scene giving it an unreal, movie-set quality. For some time Susanna stayed at Davin's side, meeting their hosts and other members of the upper echelons of the studio hierarchies. No one so far had commented on Susanna's ring, and she and Davin had agreed to wait and see how long it took for someone to do so. She drifted off to talk to some friends, two young men from the picture she had been making and a girl she had met on a previous picture. The girl noticed Susanna's ring immediately.

'What a gorgeous rock! Who's the lucky man?'

'Davin Sigmundsen,' Susanna replied, looking about in the crowd for his curly dark head, which towered above most of the men. 'We're going to announce it presently.' She smiled prettily, her eyes a little downcast.

'No kidding? I thought he and Margo Fanchon were a big item. Look over there—she's with him now.' The girl pointed and Susanna followed with her eyes to the spot indicated. Sure enough Margo Fanchon, the French actress, had her voluptuous body glued to Davin's side, her arms wound around one of his, her huge dark eyes wide and adoring as she stared up at him.

Susanna felt a knife of pure anger shoot through her. What business did that international hussy have, hanging on her man like that? Was she on the prowl again? 'Excuse me,' she said abruptly, making her way quickly through the crowd to Davin's side. She took hold of his other arm, laying her left hand conspicuously on top of it.

'Hello, darling,' she purred, smiling up at Davin with her mouth, her eyes sending another message entirely. 'I don't believe I've met your friend.'

For a moment he looked surprised at the fire in her glance, but he quickly recovered and grinned broadly. 'I'd like you to meet Margo Fanchon,' he said politely. 'Margo, my fiancée Susanna Blair. We're just about to announce our engagement publicly, I believe.'

To Margo's credit, she responded almost instantly with a happy cry and a stream of French that Susanna partly understood to mean that she was delighted for both of them.

'*Merci*,' she answered gravely, while giving Margo an A-plus for an excellent performance.

With the cat out of the bag, an announcement was soon made over the speaker system, the band played a jazzy version of the Wedding March, and lurking photographers snapped numerous pictures of the happy couple who obediently gazed at each other adoringly, kissed each other briefly, and danced together by the flower-strewn pool.

'That was mildly awful,' commented Davin as they drove home.

'Humph,' was Susanna's uncommunicative reply. She was still brooding over her response to Margo's presence at Davin's side. There had not been one shred of acting involved in her jealous anger; she did not want that woman or any other woman clutching at Davin. That realisation had haunted her for the rest of the evening, lending a brittleness to her smile and draining away some of the natural warmth with which she usually responded to Davin's nearness. 'Someone said you and Margo were an item,' she remarked, trying for a lightly casual voice.

Davin snorted. 'Silly gossip. That was a fine little jealous act you put on, though.' He looked at her appraisingly, his eyes narrowed. Her answering stare was equally penetrating.

'Academy Award quality?' she asked.

The answer was a kiss that lasted until they were home.

The week before the wedding was a pell-mell rush of activity, Susanna packing to move, the excited Maria helping, in a breathless tizzy over being one of the few invited guests to the wedding. She was thrilled, she was nervous, lapsing into frequent exclamations in her native Spanish, then pausing to translate for Susanna. Sally was even more elated, then nervous, wringing her hands lest some detail of Susanna's Victorian wedding gown be less than perfection, disappointed that she could not help choose an elaborate trousseau for the honeymoon. Blue jeans? Hiking boots?

'We're going to climb around some Mayan ruins in Yucatan,' Susanna explained patiently several times.

'No parties? No elegant resorts? Just a remote villa?'

Susanna nodded. 'We enjoy each other's company.' Which was true—very true.

Somehow during the middle of the week Davin found time to install a basketball backboard at the side of the tennis court.

'Getting ready for Bobby?' asked Susanna, as he shot a few trial baskets.

'And your brothers,' Davin answered with a grin, tossing the ball to her. She tossed a swisher through the hoop, then shrugged at Davin's open-mouthed stare.

'Little sisters learn too,' she laughed.

On Friday, Susanna was sitting at an umbrella-shaded table by the tennis court with her parents, watching

Davin and her brothers in a lively session of one-on-one at the backboard, a boisterous, happy crew, shouting and laughing. She smiled as Davin glanced over at her triumphantly as he made a slam-dunk shot. How good it was to see him looking so young and carefree, as if that sombre waxen man of the store had never even existed. She felt her mother's hand on her arm and turned to look at her.

'You've got yourself quite a man,' her mother said softly.

'I know,' Susanna agreed with a smile. 'He's very special.'

'A successful marriage takes work, especially in Hollywood, I suspect,' Mrs Blair went on, giving her daughter a searching look. She chuckled as Susanna looked away momentarily. 'Don't worry, I'm not going to give you a lecture on marriage at this late date.'

'Oh, I wasn't worried about that,' Susanna protested. She couldn't very well tell her mother that for an uncomfortable moment she had felt as if her mother could read her mind, just as she had seemed to when Susanna had been a naughty child.

'Well, something was bothering you,' Mrs Blair said with insight. 'And if it's the future of your marriage, I wouldn't fret. You already have the most important key to success.'

'What's that?' asked Susanna, her eyes drifting between her mother and the irresistible sight of Davin laughing with glee as he scored another point.

'You love him so very much,' her mother answered. 'Your face just shines with it. I'm so happy for you.'

Susanna's heart lurched, and a lump came to her throat. There it was, right in front of her, the truth she had been avoiding for days now. She did love Davin, with all her heart. It was good to be able to nod in perfectly honest agreement, her eyes aglow at the revelation she could not help but accept. 'Yes, Mother, I do—very much.'

It was even better to be able to stand before the minister the next day and make the time-honoured vows '. . . till death us do part', meaning every word. 'Till death us do part, my love,' the words sang in her heart as Davin kissed her. Somehow, Susanna vowed, she would make it come true.

CHAPTER SIX

WHEN the elation of the wedding was over, Susanna faced a sombre truth. Davin had married her for one year only, expecting her to have done the same, and it would not do for her to suddenly fling herself into his arms proclaiming her eternal love for him, begging him to make it a permanent commitment. She would have to be subtle, let things develop over time. She knew Davin was physically attracted to her, as she was to him. She could tell it in the hardness of his body as he held her close, the warmth of his lips as he kissed her, events that happened frequently during their honeymoon in the small Central American country of Belize. It would be all too easy to give in to desire, to play the seductress, giving Davin just the little extra encouragement he needed to go all the way in his lovemaking. But that would be unfair. That would be using sex to break their contract, to make Davin feel obliged to make their marriage a lasting one. Susanna was not prepared to use that tactic. No, she thought, the only right way would be to wait until a large portion of the year was up and then tell Davin, quite calmly, how she felt, hoping that by then he would have similar feelings. At least for now she must act as if their original contract were in full force.

The excitement of their honeymoon trip at first sufficiently distracted her to keep her mind off of her problem. She had never travelled outside the United States before, and finding herself in a strange and exotic tropical land was an adventure in itself. They landed at

Belize City and travelled by Land Rover to the cattle ranch of a friend of Davin's near Belmotan, the new capital of the country. Susanna found herself swivelling about constantly, exclaiming over the wild orchids blooming in the cashew trees and gasping as the driver slowed to a stop to point out a small group of wild turkeys, their luminous colours so unlike their northern brothers. The rancher had gone north with his family for a stock-buying trip, leaving his modest house available for Davin and Susanna, as well as his well-trained staff of servants who lived in thatched-roofed dwellings not far from the frame ranch house. Passing between the lush fields where herds of hump-necked, floppy-eared Brahma cattle grazed, Susanna turned to Davin and grinned,

'This is the first thing I've seen that looks anything like Iowa. Everything else is almost like another planet.'

He chuckled, 'You haven't seen anything yet!'

The ranch house was modest but spotlessly clean, a functional, working house that made Susanna feel instantly at home. If the servants thought it strange that their American guests took up residence in separate bedrooms, they did not show it, and Susanna felt sure they would not comment on it except among themselves. Davin kept them busy each day with planned excursions, inspecting the Mayan ruins of Altun Ha, hiking along mountain roads and picnicking beside tumbling waterfalls, even flying to the huge excavation of Tikal in neighbouring Guatemala, where they spent the day with an archaeologist inspecting the ancient metropolis, climbing to the tops of towering temples, and delving into the long-lost past of the vanished civilisation of the Mayans. They spent several days on the sea-coast, where Susanna learned to snorkel, diving among the coral reefs in water so clear it almost seemed like air. Not once did Davin lapse into his sullen silence, but to Susanna's tired limbs it seemed that he was determined to keep temptation at bay by exhausting them thoroughly each day. Alone in the quiet evenings they would talk about every possible topic except one. Susanna quickly discerned that there was a point in Davin's past beyond which he would not go, as if his life had begun when he took over the store after his father's death. His early childhood, she gathered, had been rather exciting, his parents travelling a great deal, but the details were sketchy. He was knowledgeable about the movie studio, but preferred leaving the details to the professionals.

'I hate dealing with artists,' he commented when Susanna asked if he would like to become more involved, a dangerous coldness in his voice. She did not pursue her enquiry.

Each evening at bedtime he would sweep her into his arms and carry her into her room, kiss her until her limbs were weak, and then leave with a soft 'good night' and a triumphant glitter in his eyes as if he were defying her to make anything more of their relationship. Susanna knew, from the response she could feel when they kissed and clung together one day on the beach, that Davin was as aroused as she. It was as if he wanted to demonstrate over and over that their physical attraction to each other had nothing to do with any deeper feelings.

On their last day at the ranch they rode out in the morning with the herdsman to inspect the cattle, then in the afternoon took the Land Rover and explored the neighbouring countryside. Davin commented enthusiastically on everything they saw, his voice a little louder than usual, his eyes unnaturally bright, as if some great fire were burning within him. His agitation communicated itself to Susanna, rubbing abrasively against her nerves, already raw from suppressing a desire that she did not really wish to quell. By evening she fell into an exhausted silence, staring out through the screened terrace into the gathering dusk. Davin sprawled beside her on a lounger, absorbed in his own thoughts. As darkness fell, he roused himself and came to stand over her, bending to pick her up.

'Time to turn in,' he said as his arms closed around her. He held her more tightly than usual, moulding her against him so that she could feel the rapid, heavy beating of his heart. Instead of setting her on her feet as he usually did when they reached her room, he carried her to her bed, sitting down with her in his arms and then stretching out beside her, his hands brushing her hair back from her fevered face, his lips crushing hers ruthlessly, demanding that she yield her mouth to his.

With a shuddering sigh she responded, her mouth opening under the onslaught, her arms stealing around to caress Davin's shoulders, feeling the tautness of his muscles as he pressed her against his length.

'Mmm,' she breathed, every thought gone as her body flamed with excitement, every point of contact aching at the barrier of clothing between them. She wanted to feel Davin's skin against hers, press her breasts against the roughness of his chest, let her fingers explore down his back and thighs. Unconsciously she tugged his knit shirt upward, and he raised up briefly and flung it aside, his eyes, dark with passion, riveting hers as he did so, daring her to move away. He unfastened her blouse, pulled off her brief shorts, and in seconds he was lying naked upon her, devouring her with kisses that left her gasping as she arched her body against him, frantic for fulfilment.

'Susanna, my lovely Susanna,' he groaned, 'I want you so desperately!'

The words hung suspended away from thought, an unreal sound that only penetrated into Susanna's consciousness as she realised that the point of no return was almost at hand. Then they crashed through, their meaning sending shudders through her body as she tried to suspend all action to give her time to think just one rational thought. He wanted her, she wanted him, it was not news, not the words she would have to hear to go on.

'I know,' she said weakly. 'Oh, Davin, I know. But aren't we forgetting something?' She jerked her head to one side, her eyes searching his face for some other words, of love and commitment, that would change the contract they had made with each other.

Davin stared at her, his breathing swift and hard, his eyes wild with frustration. His mouth hung open, and a deep, wordless growl came from his throat as he pushed himself violently away from her. Still breathing hard, his face contorted with anguish, he stood looking down at her. 'You're the one who wanted to let loose the tiger,' he rasped. 'I warned you.' Like a falling curtain of night his face became cold and impassive. Silently he snatched up his discarded clothing, turned and strode from the room.

Tears in her eyes and her heart, Susanna watched him go. 'I'm sorry,' she whispered, unheard.

The flight back to Los Angeles the next day was a nightmare for Susanna. Davin had retreated into his impenetrable shell, a shell with such perfect manners, so courteous, so charming, that only she and others who knew him well could tell there was anything amiss. It was his eyes that drove her nearly to distraction, eyes that looked at her as if she were a mannequin of skin and bone, that communicated only with the surface of life, coldly and efficiently.

'Would it help any if I apologised?' she asked desperately as the end of the flight drew near.

'No.' Davin's eyes flicked over her face. 'It's I who should apologise.' His voice was toneless, the words meaningless.

Susanna glared at him in frustration. 'It's certainly too bad you can't find some middle ground,' she snapped. 'You have no more reason to be upset than I do, and we have to face Olga in a little while. She'll know in a minute that something is wrong if you walk in looking like you just swallowed a lizard!'

Her words bounced off a stony glare. 'I'll manage,' Davin said dismissively, turning his attention to a business magazine.

Jarl met them at the airport, and if he noticed anything was amiss he was far to well trained to show it. Davin seemed to be making no effort at all to appear the happy bridegroom, assisting Susanna politely into the limousine and then taking his place by the window, staring impassively out at the passing traffic. Susanna glanced from Davin to the back of Jarl's grey head, and back again, feeling more uncomfortable by the minute. Finally she slid over next to Davin and whispered in his ear,

'Would it be asking too much for you to put your arm around me? We look like strangers sharing the same taxi.'

With a grunt, he shifted to put his arm around her, and she nestled her head against his hard shoulder, feeling the stiffened resistance of his body. She closed her eyes and pretended to sleep the rest of the way home.

Olga met them with chilled champagne to celebrate their return, her bright eyes darting piercingly from one to the other as they sat side by side on the couch in the living room and told her about the sights they had seen. Davin tried to appear jovial, and he tucked Susanna against him, toying with a lock of her hair, but Susanna could tell that Olga was not that easily fooled, as her eyes narrowed thoughtfully during Davin's description of their trip to Tikal. His narration was as impersonal as a travelogue, and it wrenched at Susanna's heart as she watched him, knowing he was trying to put on a good front and that he knew he was failing. The coldness, the fear that overtook him was not something he could discard at will, she knew that now and longed to be able to take him in her arms and kiss those fears away. That was not an approach that was likely to work, she thought with a sigh, studying the tense lines of Davin's cheek and jaw and the sculptured curve of his lips. Would he ever kiss her again?

'I'm sorry!' she said, startled, as Davin turned his head to look at her questioningly and she realised that Olga must have addressed her.

Olga smiled at her knowingly. 'I said that Cook left some sandwiches in the refrigerator for you in case you didn't have enough dinner on your flight. Are you hungry?'

'Not really. Just tired,' Susanna replied, stifling a yawn. 'Chasing this dynamo up and down ancient tombs has just about worn me out. I think I'll just turn in, if you don't mind.'

'Of course not,' Olga replied quickly. 'I'm sure you both must be tired.'

Susanna stood up and held out her hand to Davin. 'Coming, Superman?'

He nodded, looking grateful for her engineered escape, and took her hand. They bade Olga good night and started down the long hall to their room. At the door, Davin stopped and opened it, then turned away.

'I have some papers to look over in my study,' he said, after a brief glance around the room. 'Good night.' He went out, closing the door behind him, leaving Susanna standing in the middle of the huge room, bag in hand, feeling like a weary traveller abandoned by a bellboy in the wrong hotel room.

Feeling too tired to attempt to unpack, she found her soft blue velour robe and fuzzy scuffs and retreated to the luxurious bathroom. It took her several minutes to figure out how to operate the shower, and by the time she did she was almost giggling hysterically to herself at the incongruity of the situation. As the tingling fingers of the shower coursed over her she began to awaken again, her mind going over the possible alternatives for dealing with her relationship with Davin. She could just let him alone, leave him to be bottled up inside himself, keep the tiger at bay. Olga would have questions, no doubt, feel sorry for Susanna, but in the end abandon the problem as hopeless. It would be only too easy then to dissolve the marriage as unworkable. Even Bobby would probably feel the tension between them, sense that there was no permanence there. Children were surprisingly sensitive to such things, Susanna knew, the thought making her shudder as she dried herself. That poor child, of whom she still knew so little, deserved something better than that. He deserved an uncle who laughed and played with him as he had with Susanna's brothers. True, Davin would no doubt be kind and thoughtful, but . . . with an impatient gesture Susanna jerked a comb through her hair as she dried it. She was skating all around the truth again, tired as she was, avoiding the one thing that was inescapable. She loved Davin. There was only one possible course of action.

Tying her robe over a long cotton nightgown and pushing her feet into her slippers, Susanna went out of the door and down the hall towards the study.

'He's probably locked the door,' she muttered to herself, but tried the knob and, surprisingly, the door opened.

Davin was sitting hunched over his desk, his head in his hands. He did not look around as Susanna approached, although she felt sure he must have heard the door open and close. She crossed quickly to stand behind him, placing her hands on his shoulders. He whirled around, his arm slicing through the air and knocking her hands away.

'Keep your hands off me!' he grated, his eyes steely.

The blow stung and Susanna clasped her wrist, feeling a bubble of anger rising within her. Very deliberately she raised her hand and swung towards Davin's cheek, but he caught her arm in a vicelike grip and stood to tower over her, a glimmer of anger invading his mask.

'Aren't you rather overmatched?' he sneered, grasping her other arm as she attempted to poke his ribs.

'Not really,' Susanna snapped back, struggling and kicking ineffectually at his shins with her fuzzy-toed slippers. 'I just forgot my baseball bat.' She started to bring up her knee, but Davin danced back, then took her shoulders in his huge hands and shook her, his eyes now shooting bright sparks from their sea-green depths.

'What in hell is wrong with you?' he demanded, bending to peer into her flushed face.

'Nothing now,' Susanna said with a triumphant smile.

'I was just trying to get your attention. I seem to have it. We need to talk.'

Davin's hands fell to his sides, his face sagging in lines of dejection. 'If you want out of our agreement I don't blame you.'

Her eyes flew wide open in surprise. 'Want out? I want nothing of the sort. I just don't want to be married to a mummy for a year. Some people may find you charming company when you're that way, but I don't, and I don't think it's what Bobby will need either. I just want to keep my nice friendly tiger around. What do I need, a chair and a whip?'

The corners of Davin's mouth twitched a little. 'That might just be it,' he said ruefully.

Susanna eyed him narrowly. 'Maybe what you need is some other . . . sexual outlet.'

'What are you suggesting?' He glared furiously. 'That we both find some other playmate?' He clamped his hands on her shoulders again, his voice rising. 'Damn it, girl, either we're married or we're not!'

'Shhh!' warned Susanna, glancing towards the door. 'Of course that's not what I want. I just thought maybe . . . I don't want you to be miserable, that's all.'

'That's very generous of you,' Davin said dryly. He gave an immense sigh. 'I don't know the answer, Susanna, but that's not it. Hey, now what?' he asked anxiously, as tears dripped from under her downcast lashes.

All unbidden, a tremendous feeling of relief had flooded over her as she realised that she had feared Davin's withdrawal was a reaction to his knowledge that he was destined to a year of unwanted celibacy, that he was experiencing tremendous regret. Now, as he folded her close, she burrowed her cheek into his broad chest.

'I'm just glad, that's all,' she choked out, realising that from his point of view her answer probably made little sense. But then had his? She looked up and found a gentle softness in his eyes.

'I'll try harder,' he promised.

'Me too,' Susanna agreed, her lips trembling into a smile to which he responded with a tightening of his embrace and a little smile of his own.

'Shall I carry you off to bed?' he asked, starting to lift her.

'No!' she wriggled free, scowling until she caught the mischievous glint in his eyes, heard his deep, throaty chuckle. Then she too laughed as the cloak of tension slipped from her shoulders and they walked companionably, hand in hand, back to their room.

CHAPTER SEVEN

THE next morning Susanna was awakened by a soft kiss on her cheek, and her eyes flew wide open instantly to see, with a mixture of relief and regret, that Davin was standing over her, fully dressed, in a dark blue business suit.

'Good morning, sleepyhead,' he said with a smile, holding out towards her a cup of coffee. 'Need some help waking up?'

'Mmmm, that smells heavenly,' smiled Susanna, sitting up and pushing her hair back from her face, unaware of how desirable she looked in her pink-cheeked, tousled condition. Davin handed her the coffee and beat a retreat halfway to the door.

'I've got to get to the office and see if the store is still solvent,' he said. 'I already called the Winters. We can pick Bobby up next Sunday afternoon.'

'Oh, good.' Susanna puckered her brow thoughtfully. 'What day is today? I seem to have lost track of time.'

He consulted his elegant gold chronograph. 'Today is Monday, August 15th,' he reported.

'Goodness! We'll just have time to get Bobby settled before he has to register for school. Would you like me to do something about his room?' The room that was destined to be Bobby's was, at present, decorated in a decidedly feminine style, floral prints in the curtains and bedspread, white lacquered furniture, a fluffy white rug.

'I'll make a list today,' said Davin, turning towards the door. 'We can go over it tonight.'

'Davin,' Susanna called out, her voice lilting silkily, 'you could leave it up to me, you know. You already have enough to do, and I do know what boys like. I even have a pretty good idea what you would like.' She paused and smiled persuasively as Davin pulled thoughtfully on his chin. 'Unless, of course,' she added, 'it means a great deal to you to be in on it.'

He shook his head. 'Not really. You go ahead—do anything you like.' He grinned wickedly. 'I keep forgetting you're not as dumb as your blonde beauty would indicate.'

'Oooh!' Susanna growled, rising to the bait. 'You male chauvinist!' She subsided into giggles, as Davin left with a wink and a wave, chuckling to himself.

Olga was lingering over her tea in the breakfast room, a room with curved glass walls overlooking the pool but she sheltered from its glare by a latticework canopy hung with trailing begonias. She gave Susanna a warmly welcoming smile.

'Davin seemed in a much better humour this morning,' she observed, a twinkle in her bright blue eyes.

Susanna's cheeks felt warm, but she smiled back. 'Yes,' she agreed and then quickly changed the subject. 'He said I could go ahead and fix up Bobby's room. I'll have to get cracking on that. We're to pick him up on Sunday.'

'I might be able to help you on that,' suggested Olga. 'I used to do a bit of . . . decorating myself.'

'Oh, did you?' Susanna smiled a thanks at the maid who brought her more coffee and a poisonously rich-looking pastry. Then her mind suddenly clicked in on Olga's words and she paused with her coffee cup halfway to her mouth. 'A bit of . . . set decorating?' she asked in a hushed voice. Olga's smile was answer enough. 'Oh, my . . .' Susanna put her hand to her forehead, 'I don't know why . . . you're the famous . . . oh, why didn't I guess it?' Under the single name of 'Olga', this elderly lady had been one of the most famous of the early designers in Hollywood.

'Probably because Davin led you to believe I'm such a stodgy old fossil,' replied Olga with a chuckle.

'Oh, he didn't . . .' Susanna began, but Olga silenced her with a graceful, bejewelled wave of her hand.

'Never mind. He's a dear boy and he means well,' she said. 'Now, shall we call Jarl to bring the limousine around? It's so handy for carrying parcels, and we'll no doubt have quite a lot.'

'That would be fine,' Susanna agreed, feeling quite swept along by this eighty-year-old dynamo. She felt even more so a few hours later, for Olga zipped from store to store, obviously quite familiar with their stocks and friendly with the owners. She had definite ideas about what she wanted, especially after Susanna asked her about Bobby's likes and dislikes and Olga replied that he was very fond of wild animals.

'I think he'd like to live at the zoo,' Olga told her, 'so perhaps we ought to go with a wild animal theme of some sort.'

'I think that would be terrific,' Susanna replied. 'My brothers would have loved that.' She took the opportunity to ask a few more questions about Bobby, for Davin had told her very little after their first encounter.

'He's bright and active,' Olga told her, 'but he needs to have some friends his own age. Poor boy hasn't had much chance for that.' In response to Susanna's query about his appearance, Olga replied, 'He looks just like his father.' That was not much help, Susanna thought to herself, since she had never seen a picture of Carl. He must have looked something like Davin, though, being his brother, so Bobby no doubt would too.

By the end of the morning Susanna was exhausted, but Olga was still going strong. 'You certainly know exactly what's available,' Susanna remarked, as she sank with relief into the cushions of the limousine. 'I can't believe all your decorating is in the past.'

'Smart girl,' Olga said with a twinkling smile. 'I still do quite a bit for old friends, and their families. They like my price . . . free.'

'Olga!' Susanna scolded. 'You shouldn't! Or is there a reason? Davin . . . does he know you do it?'

'I'm sure he must, but we both pretend I don't.'

'But why?'

'It's a long story I'll tell you some day,' Olga said dryly. 'Suffice it to say that Davin prefers to pretend some things are not as they are.' She said no more on the subject, and Susanna was left to wonder what other things Davin was pretending about, wishing desperately that she could pry into the subject further for clues about his periods of darkness but knowing that Olga would only tell her when she felt the time was right.

Workmen appeared as if by magic in response to Olga's calls, and by Thursday afternoon Bobby's room had been transformed into a small corner of the jungle, with a huge photo mural of a real jungle on one wall, some fake animal skins against the darkly leafy wallpaper, shaggy tiger-skin spreads of acrylic on the beds, palm fronds on the curtains, and a real potted palm in one corner. A boy who loved wild animals would be sure to love it, Susanna thought, and she could hardly wait for Davin to come home to show him the results.

*   *   *

Davin had been in such a good humour lately that Susanna was completely unprepared for the dark look of disgust, almost hatred, that replaced his eager smile when he saw the room. He stood with his hands on his hips, his lip curled in distaste, as he looked around the room.

'If this isn't true Hollywood,' he snarled, impaling Susanna with a cold and bitter stare. 'Are you out of your mind? Or . . . do I detect the fine hand of dear Olga at work? That's it, isn't it?' he asked rhetorically as Susanna swallowed and paled before his icy stare.

'She . . . did help me a little,' she replied, 'but . . .'

'Get rid of it,' he ordered, with a sweeping gesture. 'All the boy needs is a nice, simple, plain room.'

'But there isn't time!' Susanna cried.

'Then perform a miracle,' said Davin in clipped tones. 'Make time.' He turned to go.

'Now just a darn minute,' she snapped, fury and frustration making her eyes flash above her defiantly lifted chin. 'It may be a little . . . overdone, but I refuse to hurt Olga's feelings by doing it all over. I . . . I'll paint the walls a nice plain colour, but that's all I'll do.' She scowled into the forbidding, frozen green of Davin's eyes.

'Very well,' he said stiffly. 'And get rid of all the arty folderol.' He gestured towards the animal skins and the palm tree, then marched brusquely from the room.

Damn, Susanna thought, her heart sinking as she watched the broad, rigid back retreating. Just when she had thought things were on an even keel . . . but she might have known Davin would want something more simple. She should have held Olga back, but it had been such fun . . .

Dinner that night was strained, Davin silent and

withdrawn, not looking at either Olga or Susanna except when spoken to, his answers short and barely polite.

'He didn't like the wallpaper,' she answered in response to Olga's whispered query, but she could tell by Olga's expression that the elderly woman guessed far more than that was amiss.

Davin did not come to his bed that night, apparently spending the night on the couch in his study. Susanna could not sleep, torn between a desire to try to jolt him out of his withdrawal and a simmering anger at his unreasonableness. She tried to put together her scanty clues to figure out the basis for his irrational response. The first few times he had become cold and withdrawn she had not noticed any particular reason for it. Then in Belize, it had been obvious that it was frustration and rejection that had set him off. But what on earth did art and Hollywood and Olga's decorating have to do with it? There must be some way to put it all together, but hours of puzzling in between periods of fitful dozing brought Susanna no closer to an answer. By dawn she finally fell into a deep sleep, and when she awakened again Davin had apparently sneaked in and out of the room, and had gone off again for the day.

She felt tired, fuzzy-headed, and entirely out of sorts. She skipped breakfast in order to avoid confronting Olga in her ill-humoured state, and hurried to a paint store where she purchased several gallons of a light beige paint and the brushes and rollers to do the job herself. It was far too late to hire someone, and besides, she had done plenty of painting herself before. No use acting like one of the idle rich, since she was obviously never going to have a chance to become one of them, she thought grimly as she spread a drop cloth over the furniture and yanked the animal skins from the walls. It was one thing to love a warm, wonderful, passionate man, but there was no way a person could spend their life being buffeted between joy and despair every few days.

'I'd look a hundred years old by the time I was forty,' she muttered to herself as she tugged the beds away from the walls and spread another cover over the soft green carpet. Davin Sigmundsen was just going to have to find someone else to cope with his volatile moods. Not that he hadn't planned to, anyway . . . She set to work with a steely set to her jaw, watching the beautiful wallpaper disappear behind the plain, light-coloured paint. She had just finished the longest wall and was standing on a chair to paint along the ceiling of another when a deep voice said in flat, dull tones,

'We could afford to hire someone to do that, you know.'

Susanna turned to look at the tall, elegantly dressed man standing in the doorway. 'Too short notice,' she said, making her own voice as cold and unemotional as his. 'Besides, I'm quite capable of doing it. I painted my own apartment.' She turned abruptly back to her task, expecting further argument, but got none. When she looked again, Davin was gone. He reappeared minutes later, dressed in jeans and an old sweatshirt.

'Let me,' he said, reaching for the paintbrush.

'No,' she replied, and felt herself lifted bodily from the chair.

'I won't need a chair,' Davin said, and took the paintbrush from her hand with unmistakable firmness, quickly demonstrating the truth of his statement.

'I always did wish I was taller,' Susanna grumbled at his back. 'I'll do the roller part.'

Davin made no reply, silently outlining the ceiling, doorway and windows, while Susanna began filling in with the roller. She tried to make conversation, but got brief, monotonal replies:

'You're home early.'

'It's Friday.'

'How's Sally?'

'Fine.'

'Is this colour all right?'

'It will do.'

In spite of herself, Susanna felt her heart begin to melt. The lines of tension around Davin's eyes and mouth were those of an unhappy man, and she could not bear to see him unhappy. Perhaps she could jolly him out of it.

'Davin . . . I'm sorry you didn't like the room,' she said gently, 'but it seemed like a perfect room for the nephew of a tiger.'

In response, he gave her a blank, glassy look, his mouth still tightened into an unresponsive line.

'So be in a lousy mood,' Susanna muttered unhappily, filling her roller with more than adequate vigour, the paint splashing on to the dropcloth.

'Be more careful,' Davin said brusquely, surveying the little mess. 'We're painting the walls, not the floor.'

'Maybe you are,' she growled back, her ill-temper returning as her frustration grew. 'I'm more creative.' As he looked up stonily from where he had bent to get more paint, she calmly reached out with her roller and made a complete sweep over half of his face. 'You might as well *look* like a mummy,' she ground out through clenched teeth, as Davin's eyes blinked once in disbelief and then turned into pools of wild emerald sparks.

'You crazy idiot!' he exclaimed, rising to tower hugely over her. He grabbed for a cloth and began wiping at his face, his hand trembling in reflection of his rage.

'Susanna,' he choked out, his chest heaving, 'one of these times you are going to go too far!'

'And that will be only a few minutes after *you* have,' she replied, jerking her chin up defiantly, trembling inside at the sight of six and a half feet of enraged masculinity in spite of her relief at seeing emotion crack the cage of ice in which Davin had been trapped. 'I'm getting a little tired of this routine,' she went on as he continued to stare at her as if she had lost her mind. 'I can't go through life carrying a baseball bat.' She looked him straight in the eyes, her face apparently calm, although her heart was pounding as he raised a clenched fist, then opened his hand and dropped his head against it, standing as still as a statue for what seemed like an eternity.

'Isn't it easier than a whip and a chair?' he asked at last, his voice husky. He raised his head, looking at Susanna with a face transformed into gentle concern, soft sea-green eyes so wistful that the love and tenderness she felt in response shook her to her very toes. She could only shake her head and blink tear-misted eyes in reply, then cling fiercely to the massive back as he reached out and swept her into his arms.

'I ought to be horsewhipped,' he murmured as he felt her small body trembling against his.

'Shall I try that next time?' asked Susanna, nestling limply against his chest, wanting only to stay close to this strange but wonderful man for ever.

'There won't be a next time,' he said gruffly. He raised her face with his hand. 'There are some things I may not be reasonable about . . . art and artists in particular . . . but I'll try to remember to yell and curse and throw things in the future, if that's what you'd prefer.'

'I would,' she replied, drowning happily in the warmth

of his embrace, as his lips curved into a smile that sent songbirds fluttering through her heart. 'I don't know why, but I can't bear it when you turn to stone.'

'I couldn't bear it if you did,' he replied. 'I think I understand.' Slowly, almost reluctantly, he caressed her cheek, then cradled her head in his huge hand and lowered his own, his mouth soft and warm and still tasting of paint as he kissed her with such passion that she felt faint, the real world melding with one all made of light and fire and deep longings as they tasted each other with fierce delight and their bodies pressed together in unspoken confession of forbidden desire. But it was forbidden, and Susanna withdrew her mouth from Davin's and ran a finger lightly across his lips.

'You taste like sand beige semi-gloss wall enamel,' she said between teasing nibbles at his lips with her own.

'That's not my fault.' Davin's mouth moved over her face, his teeth tugged tenderly at her earlobe. 'You taste like sugar and spice.' His mouth returned to cover hers briefly, then he drew back and held her a little away from him. 'Thank you, Susanna,' he said softly.

'Any time,' she whispered, sure that in her eyes he could read her heart saying over and over, 'Davin, I love you so much'. Afraid that she would say it aloud, she smiled shakily. 'I think I'm beginning to like that effect,' she said. 'You ought to look in the mirror. It's really quite fetching.'

Davin walked into the adjoining bath. 'You're right. I think I'll leave it this way,' he said with a grin that creased through the paint. 'We're going to the store later on. It will be interesting to see how Sally likes it.'

'I was only joking,' Susanna said as she began filling the basin with warm water. 'Sit down so I can clean you up, and then tell me why we're going to the store.'

'Because,' said Davin, grimacing as she rubbed vigorously with a wash cloth, 'unless I'm mistaken, you'll never take me up on my offer unless I drag you down there, and we have several parties coming up, not the least of which is Olga's bash tomorrow night. I told Sally to find some suitable things, and I have something in mind myself.'

'Oh, Davin,' Susanna scolded, without much conviction, 'I don't really need anything new.' But as a look of fleeting but deep sadness crossed his face she threw her arms around him and kissed his now clean lips. 'That was just a reflex,' she told him with a comforting hug. 'My parents taught me not to be greedy, but I would dearly love some beautiful new clothes. I'm just afraid you'll spoil me.'

He pulled her on to his lap and smiled at her affectionately. 'I think that would be well nigh impossible,' he said, 'but if I see it happening, I'll paint you green.'

'Paint me the colour of your eyes,' Susanna suggested. 'It's beautiful.' She smiled back into the lovely clearness of sunlight on the sea, but in her heart she was troubled still. What terrible thing could have hurt this man so deeply? Had someone forced him to give up his own art, that once perhaps meant his very life to him? Had some cruel critic rejected it, told him it was worthless? When she had momentarily demurred at his offer of the treasures of his fabulous store he had responded as if she had rejected a part of him. She must be very careful never to do that again. Then maybe someday he would tell her . . . She sighed and buried her cheek against his throat, hugging him fiercely again, wishing desperately there were some way she could erase whatever had caused him such pain.

'Something wrong?' he asked, sensitive as always to her mood.

'Hmm-mmm,' Susanna replied, 'but I'm afraid I'm getting addicted to all this hugging and kissing and it isn't getting the painting done.'

He sighed also then and carefully stood her on her feet. 'I'm afraid we were both taught never to start something we couldn't finish,' he said dryly. He looked at his watch. 'We may have to finish the painting in the morning. I told Sally we'd be there by three. On the other hand . . .' he looked at the room, with three walls already painted and only the mural wall left to do, 'we might just leave that mural. It's really not so bad, once you get rid of the other junk, is it?'

'No. I kind of like it, especially that tiger over there.' She pointed to the great beast lurking behind a tree. It was an attractive photograph, but there was a certain former artist she knew who could do a great deal better. This certainly wasn't the time to bring that up, though, she thought, chewing on her lip meditatively.

'You don't really like it,' Davin said perceptively.

'Oh, no!' Susanna said quickly. 'It's fine.'

'Susanna!' he said in a deep, warning tones, although he smiled at the same time. 'What's the problem?'

She felt a nervous shiver run through her as she looked into his eyes. She just wasn't any good at lying, but if she told him what she had been thinking . . . 'I . . . I was thinking . . .' She stopped, unwilling to precipitate another crisis.

'Out with it, Susanna,' Davin said firmly. 'I won't bite, I promise.'

'Well,' she said weakly, 'I thought you could do better.'

He looked momentarily startled, then he took a deep

breath and smiled, giving her pale cheek a gentle caress. 'Maybe . . . some time,' he said slowly. 'Maybe sometime.' Those three simple, reluctant words were, Susanna realised, a greal deal for Davin to say.

Susanna was so euphoric, both over Davin's very apparent happiness the rest of the afternoon and over the prospect of actually owning some of the fabulous clothes she had once modelled, that she babbled excitedly on the way to the store.

'Calm down, woman,' ordered Davin, his delighted grin belying his scolding tone. 'You're worse than a kid at Christmas!'

'I can't help it,' Susanna replied, 'that's how I feel. I never even let myself imagine the clothes I modelled were mine. I had to learn when I was little not to want things we couldn't afford. This is like finding out there really is a Santa Claus.' She gave him a sideways glance. 'You do promise you won't disappear up the chimney later, don't you?'

'Absolutely,' he said seriously, 'if you promise you won't disappear on the stroke of midnight.'

'I promise,' she said quickly. Then a thought made her heart do a flip-flop and start racing. Had Davin meant anything more than a lighthearted reference to another fairy tale? She looked over at his handsome profile and he turned his head to give her a warm glance that sent her heart to speeding even faster. It took her several minutes to convince her love-racked emotions to be more calm and sensible, and accept his remark for something less than a declaration of some new commitment. Surely, if Davin wanted to change things, he would come right out and say so, she warned herself. Don't build castles of sand. She was still trying to untie her inner knots when Sally greeted her with a vigorous hug and a delighted chuckle.

'My goodness, how marriage does agree with you!' she smiled, surveying Susanna's bright eyes and flushed cheeks. 'You look like *several* million. And just wait till you see what I've got for you to try on!'

Sally's bubbling enthusiasm soon had Susanna's excitement rekindled, and she giggled irrepressibly when Sally nearly fainted at the sight of Davin dressed in tight jeans and a bright yellow shirt that set off his dark red hair and deep California tan.

'Good heavens, Mr Sigmundsen,' Sally exclaimed, her eyes popping wide open. 'I never saw you . . . in . . . dressed like that before!' It was obvious that she was overwhelmed by the vital sexuality he exuded in such attire, with a relaxed grin on his striking face.

'Susanna's influence,' he replied with a wink, before he turned his attention to the rack of clothes Sally had prepared. 'Where's the jacket?' he asked.

'It's on the way,' Sally answered, leaving Susanna to wonder what on else there could possibly be, for the selection she saw was nothing short of fantastic.

'Okay, ladies,' said Davin, turning to go to the salon. 'Let the show begin.'

'Now I see what you saw,' Sally said, rolling her eyes as he left the dressing room, and Susanna laughed and blushed. If Sally only knew!

Sally's unerring eye had picked out more than a dozen assorted dresses for Susanna to try, and every one was lovely in its own special way. There was a black silk cocktail dress, slender and sophisticated; a rose-coloured afternoon dress of fine Italian wool, draped at an angle, with long sleeves; a blue silk suit with shoes to match; long gowns of ivory lace, yellow chiffon, a blue velvet with a fur-trimmed jacket, and Susanna's favourite, an amethyst chiffon with a skirt like layers of petals. To go with this, Sally brought out an amethyst choker and earrings.

'That gorgeous man of yours is going to like this,' she predicted.

Susanna made a face at her, but her eyes were lighted with a special brightness as she danced across the floor towards Davin. Yes, she thought with a quick intake of breath as she smiled at him, he is a gorgeous man. Her heart began pounding in an unruly fashion as he stood up and moved towards her, his eyes holding hers with a gentle warmth. He stopped in front of her and put his hands on her bare shoulders.

'I think that dress must have been made just for you,' he said softly. 'It makes your eyes look like two wild violets.' His hands slid around her back, his mouth coming down on to hers, tentatively at first as if testing her response, then possessively as he felt her melt into his arms, her lips parting eagerly as her head began to spin, flinging the real world away. It was almost as if he were *her* gorgeous man . . . almost. As Davin drew his head back and still held her close, she rested her head against his hard chest, listening to the heavy, strong beat of his heart. Her arms were tight around his back, never wanting to let him go.

'Oh, Davin,' she murmured huskily, 'I don't . . .'

'Shhh,' he said, his lips against her hair. 'I don't want any thanks. Seeing you look so beautiful and happy is enough.'

Susanna nodded silently, choking back the tears that sprang to her eyes. She had not been going to thank him. She had been going to tell him, foolishly, that she did not think she could live without him. With a shudder of relief at being saved from making such a terrible mistake she pulled back and looked up at him with a wistful little smile.

'May I just say, Mr Sigmundsen,' she said lightly, 'that you are the most terrific husband I've ever had?'

'You may,' Davin replied, taking her face between his huge hands and giving her another quick kiss, 'if I may return the compliment, terrific wife.' There was a seriousness about his face, a deep-fathomed sparkle to his sea-green eyes and a yearning curve to his sensuous mouth that made Susanna's heart begin to race once more. Surely there was a depth of affection there that might give her hope that something lasting would grow between them, if only she could keep from trying to push things too fast. A polite cough brought them both back to reality.

'Here's the jacket, Mr Sigmundsen,' said Sally, advancing towards them, a fur over her arm. 'The furrier just delivered it.'

'Ah, yes,' Davin said with a satisfied smile, taking it from her and holding it out for Susanna to put on.

Wide-eyed, Susanna slipped into the hip-length jacket of softest chinchilla, reflexively pulling the luscious creation close around her. It was a dream, light and warm and incredibly elegant.

'That *was* made especially for you,' Davin told her, chuckling at her expression of complete amazement.

'Oh, Davin . . .' Tears welled up and rolled down Susanna's cheeks, tears of gratitude for his thoughtfulness, but most of all tears of pain, for she wanted so much to tell Davin that she loved him that it hurt with a terrible ache not to do so.

'Now don't drip all over it,' Sally chided gently, handing Susanna a Kleenex. 'I'm afraid you've overwhelmed her, Mr Sigmundsen.'

'No more than she's overwhelmed me,' he replied, watching Susanna with a bemused expression as she dabbed at her eyes and brought a wavering smile to her lips. 'You should see this lady when she really goes into action,' he added, his teasing smile succeeding in lightening Susanna's mood.

'Now don't you go telling tales,' she retorted, 'just because you need a little stirring up now and then!'

'Okay, he replied agreeably, 'but you'd better get back into your jeans. My stomach tells me it's feeding time at the zoo. Sally, send everything out on the truck tomorrow.'

'Everything?' croaked Susanna.

'Yes, everything,' Davin affirmed. 'Now get a move on, woman,' he added with a grin as she still stared at him, speechless.

With a shake of her head she roused herself. 'All right, chubby,' she said archly, giving a playful poke at his rock-hard midriff, then scurrying to escape as he tried to spank her backside.

'You don't know how lucky you are to have a man who loves you so much,' Sally said wistfully as she took the chinchilla from Susanna and caressed it with longing fingers. 'He looks at you as if he'd just like to . . . eat you up.'

'Oh, Sally!' Susanna protested, her immediate thought not of the implications of Sally's words for herself but of the sadness she saw on the older woman's face. She slipped out of the amethyst gown and went to put her arm around Sally's shoulders. 'If anyone deserves a fine man, it's you,' she said warmly. 'You do so much for others, and you're such a good companion. One will come along soon, I'd bet my life on it.'

'Hmmph,' Sally snorted, trying for her usual bravado. 'You're crazy to make a bet like that with my track record. I seem to scare them away as fast as I find them.'

'Then I'll put in an order for one who's not such a coward,' Susanna promised, vowing to herself that she would keep her eyes open among the new people she was sure to meet in the months ahead. It was not until she lay in bed later that night, listening to Davin's regular breathing as he lay asleep in the other big bed, that she remembered what Sally had said about Davin's obvious love for her. Could Sally be right? Did she really see something there, or was it just her frustrated imagination? She sighed and buried her face in her pillow. Probably the latter, she told herself, trying to squelch the flickering fire of longing before it became a flame that consumed her.

CHAPTER EIGHT

'DID you enjoy the party last night?' Davin asked as they drove south towards Huntington Beach on Sunday afternoon. He had been silent most of the way, and Susanna had been content to leave him so, for she was still sleepy. Olga's 'bash' had proved to be one of the most interesting and exciting parties she had ever attended, lasting well into the wee hours of the morning.

'It was fantastic,' she replied. 'It was like having a front row seat for the history of Hollywood. Olga must know everyone who's ever been important in the history of the movies. I never expected to see all those people, let alone meet them.'

Davin chuckled. 'I see she properly impressed you! But you're right, it was a fabulous crowd. It makes you realise how short the history of motion pictures is, though, doesn't it? There were people there who knew Chaplin and Harold Lloyd well, who made silent films as well as talkies. They've seen it all.'

'I was shaking in my slippers when Olga introduced us,' Susanna said, laughing as she remembered the lavish compliment. Olga had rung a tinkling bell when Davin and Susanna appeared, calling the whole crowd to attention, then introducing them as 'the best looking couple since Gable and Lombard.'

'I'm just surprised she didn't hire a trumpeter to play a fanfare,' Davin said dryly. 'And actually, I'm not sure I like being compared to Gable. My ears aren't that big.'

'Don't complain,' Susanna teased. 'He's still my all-time favourite.'

He grinned. 'You're better looking than Lombard,' he said, casting a glance at her that made her blush and her heart beat faster. He had been so warm and devoted to her the previous evening, it was hard to believe that it was only an act. She sighed and looked over at him, but he was once again staring straight ahead, his mind apparently far away.

Memories, Susanna thought. There must be many memories involved in this day when he became, at least in name, the father of his only brother's son. Her own life had been so deeply entwined with her two beloved brothers that her heart would be broken at the loss of either of them. How hard she would try, if it were her place to do so, to be a good parent to a little niece or nephew left in her charge. Davin had still told her very little about Bobby, but perhaps that was just as well. She was free to form her own impressions of the boy, un-impeded by others' opinions.

They turned off the ocean-front highway, Davin guiding the car through a series of turns until they came to a street of small stuccoed houses, all more or less alike, except for the fact that some were well maintained while others were in decided need of paint and repair. The shiny Mercedes looked woefully out of place among the many dilapidated cars and motorcycles that cluttered the street and driveways.

'Here we are,' said Davin, pulling into the drive of a shabby-looking house with a lawn that was little more than a weed patch, made even more disreputable-looking by several discarded beer cans lying beneath the straggly bushes next to the front steps. He did not get out, but sat with his hands on the wheel, staring straight ahead, his angular face taut and pale.

Susanna put her hand on his. 'Nervous?' she asked quietly.

Davin nodded. 'A little.'

'You don't think the Winters will back out, do you?'

'No, not really . . . but it's like . . . every Christmas and birthday I ever had, all rolled into one, and . . . I'm almost afraid to believe it's going to happen.' He looked over at Susanna, his eyes misty. 'Did you ever feel like that?'

'Oh, yes. Especially at Christmas. When I was little I routinely made myself sick with worry by December the twentieth. My mother used to tell me to ask Santa for a better stomach!'

He gave her a strange look and buried his face in his hands, his shoulders shaking.

'Oh, Davin, I'm sorry!' Susanna cried, feeling close to tears at the thought that she had made too light of his deep emotions.

He lowered his hands, revealing eyes sparkling with laughter. 'I was just picturing poor little Susanna, all pale and greenish beneath the Christmas tree.' His mouth curved into a boyish grin.

'As long as it makes you happy,' she said primly, then burst into giggles as he roared with laughter.

'Come on,' he said, opening his door to get out. 'Far better Bobby should be welcomed by such a jolly pair.'

It was hard to stay jolly, though, for at the sound of the car doors closing a heavy-set man dressed in a faded plaid shirt and sagging blue jeans came out of the front door and walked towards them a little unsteadily. His eyes were bleary and his face bore the unhealthy flush of a heavy drinker.

'Bobby'll be out in a minute,' he said in a wheezy

voice. 'Mom's saying goodbye to him inside. She's taking this pretty hard, you know.' He cast a baleful glare at Davin and then turned cold, watery eyes on Susanna. 'So you're the little movie dolly he's latched on to,' he said, jerking his head towards Davin as he spoke. 'Don't look to me like you'll make much of a mother for our grandson.'

Out of the corner of her eye Susanna could see Davin's face grow dark with anger, and she quickly smiled and held out her hand towards Mr Winters. 'I'm really just a girl from a little country town in Iowa,' she said firmly, 'and I grew up with two brothers, so I know quite a bit about the tricks little boys are full of. My name is Susanna.'

'That your real name?' the man asked suspiciously as he wiped his hand on the side of his trousers and took hers reluctantly.

'Yes.' Susanna almost winced at the hard, rough grip of the old man's hand. He gave her a sly smile.

'You ain't slow, that's for sure,' he said as he dropped her hand and darted a look at Davin, who was regaining control of his anger, his jaw set and his mouth in a rigid line. 'You've got more sense than I thought,' the man wheezed in a backhanded compliment.

Davin did not reply, for at that moment the door opened again and a short, elderly lady appeared, tears streaming unchecked down her wrinkled cheeks as she clutched at the arm of a tall, gangly boy who was already several inches taller than she.

Susanna caught her breath as the boy turned to look towards them, his face breaking into a wide grin as he spied Davin. If Bobby looked like his father, then Davin and his brother must have been as alike as two peas. The same dark red hair was his, the high cheekbones, the eyes that sparkled green beneath their rusty lashes. The nose and chin were still those of a boy, but promised to become duplicates of Davin's with maturity. It was with deeply conflicting emotions that Susanna realised how easy it would be to fall head over heels in love with this boy, even as she had with his uncle. She could not take her eyes from him, as he tore himself from his grandmother's grasp and ran across the little yard to where Davin now waited with a look of utter joy, his arms outstretched towards the younger version of himself.

'You won't forget your old grandma, will you?' came a plaintive voice as Mrs Winters hobbled arthritically down the steps, brushing the tears angrily from her cheeks as if they offended her.

'Of course he won't,' Davin said impatiently, and Susanna cast him a reproachful glance. The old woman was obviously as well acquainted with the bottle as her husband, but her grief was genuine.

'We'll keep in touch,' Susanna promised.

'He'll never come back,' the woman wailed. 'We'll never see him again! Those terrible Sigmundsens—first they took my little Elena and now they're taking my little Bobby. There's nothing left for me any more, nothing left!'

'We'll bring him to visit you often,' Susanna tried to reassure her, but the poor woman wailed on, so deeply locked into her agonising that she seemed not to see or hear anything else.

Mr Winters nodded at Susanna as if to say he would take care of things. 'Come on, Mama,' he said gently, putting his arm around her. 'You come and get a little drink and watch the baseball game on television. You'll feel better in a little while.' Without another word he led the still sobbing woman into the house and closed the door. Susanna watched them go with an ache in her heart both for the elderly couple and for what Bobby must have endured with them.

'Susanna?' Davin's voice startled her and she turned to look at the other pair. There was no sorrow there, only a deep contentment. Their agony was over.

'Hello, Bobby,' smiled Susanna, holding out her hand to him.

'Hi, Susanna,' Bobby replied a little shyly, his mouth curving into the same delicious lines as Davin's did when he smiled. He gave her hand a little squeeze. 'She's not so bad when she's sober,' he said, with that tolerant sophistication of the young who have had to cope with such problems. 'I think she had a little extra today because I was leaving.'

'I expect so,' Susanna agreed.

Bobby's duffle bag was tossed into the trunk of the car and then Davin invited him to sit in front with him. 'Susanna won't mind riding in the back,' he said, and so they started on the trip back to Bel Air. For a time they kept up a lively three-way conversation, but after a while Susanna fell silent, watching the two in the front seat. It was so obvious that they belonged together. Davin must have spent quite a lot of time with the boy to have built up such a good relationship with him. There was nothing in their behaviour towards one another to suggest that Bobby had ever been subjected to the coldly withdrawn man Susanna had first known as Davin Sigmundsen. But then children and puppies can sometimes penetrate barriers that adults are helpless to cross.

They came to a stop light and while they waited for it to change, Davin turned his head towards Bobby and the boy looked up at his uncle. As she saw their two profiles, like two beautifully etched coins against the outside light, Susanna's breath caught in her throat for a second time that afternoon, another ache invaded her heart. Here she was, already relegated to the back seat, the outsider, her mission fulfilled. At that morose thought she bit her lip, catching sight of her downcast expression in a passing car window. Good lord, I'm as pitiful as Mrs Winters, she thought grimly. Straighten up, Susanna. You're not a back-seat sort of person. Resolutely replacing her drooping mouth with a smiling one, she leaned forward and placed her elbows on the seat back between the two.

'Would anyone besides me like some ice cream?' she enquired, laughing as both Davin and Bobby turned smiling faces towards her and said a hearty, 'Yes!'

'How do you like your new stepson?' asked Davin that night as they retired to their room after having received crushing good night hugs from a very happy Bobby.

'You have to ask?' Susanna chided gently. 'I think he's terrific.'

'Yes, he is,' Davin agreed, giving her a warm smile, 'in spite of everything. He thinks you're terrific too.'

'If he's going to keep thinking so I'm going to have to get in shape,' said Susanna with a grimace. They had gone swimming before dinner and played basketball afterwards in an attempt to help Bobby wear off some of his nervous energy.

Davin grinned. 'I know what you mean,' he said, rubbing his back and groaning in exaggerated pain. 'I'm ten years older than you are and feeling every minute of it.'

'Poor old thing,' Susanna teased, giving him a sympathetic pat, 'why don't you take your shower first? The hot water will help.'

While Davin showered, she sat on the end of her bed, lost in thought. It had been a fine day, a wonderful one for Davin, but seeing Bobby . . . there was no way she could help but love him. They were so alike. If leaving Davin would have been terribly hard, leaving the two of them would be well nigh impossible, and not just because of her own sorrow. It would be unthinkable to hurt that gangling awkward-puppy of a boy, whose bright, searching eyes and ready smile revealed to Susanna's sensitive nature a desperate eagerness for love and security. She had thought to hold back a little, perhaps not become too deeply involved, but that had become instantly impossible. She had thought perhaps Davin would have the same idea, but if he had he must have abandoned it immediately also. There was nothing to do not but go forward, one day at a time.

When she had finished bathing and putting on her nightgown and robe she found Davin lying in his bed, his hands beneath his head as he stared at the ceiling. His face, so happy only a short time ago, looked drawn and worried.

'What's wrong, Davin?' she asked, coming to stand above him. Was he, too, becoming concerned about the complication of Bobby's presence to their agreement? she wondered, but found that was not the reason for his sad expression as he reached out and took her hand, coaxing her to sit on the edge of his bed.

'Just feeling guilty,' he answered. 'We have so much now, and the Winters have so little.'

'That's not your fault,' she said gently. 'You can't be blamed for their alcoholism or the death of their daughter.'

Davin tightened his lips and sighed. 'Not directly . . . but I wish I could help them somehow. I feel so helpless.'

'I guess that's a common feeling,' Susanna said slowly. 'That's why there are support groups like Alanon and Alateen for the families of alcoholics. There's really nothing you can do unless they want to help themselves.'

'Still . . .' Davin fretted, chewing his lower lip.

'Have you tried talking to them directly about their drinking?' asked Susanna. As Davin shook his head she went on, 'It probably wouldn't help, but you never know. You could at least give it a try, let them know you're ready to help any way you can. You'd feel better if you did.'

'I'll do that,' he said, but he still looked sad, the earlier sparkle gone from his sea-green eyes, leaving them flat and dull-looking.

The day had rekindled too many memories, Susanna guessed. Poor Davin—just when he should have been most happy. 'We can't bring Carl or Elena back,' she said, 'but we can make sure the Winters see their grandson often.'

Davin nodded silently again.

'What was she like?' she asked.

'Very lovely . . . to look at,' he answered, a darkness crossing his face, making her wish she had not asked. Had Elena's virtues perhaps not matched her beauty, a beauty that had lured Carl into an unhappy marriage? Susanna was curious, but she could not pursue that subject now. She reached out and caressed Davin's hair back from his forehead.

'Why don't you try thinking about what we're going to do with that eleven-year-old superman until school starts?' she suggested, trying to get Davin to focus on the present instead of the past.

'I've got a lot of plans for that,' he replied. He shifted restlessly, then gave her an almost pleading look.

'Would you do something for me, Susanna?'

'Of course,' she answered without hesitation.

He moved and threw his covers back. 'Let me hold you for a while,' he said huskily, a crooked, apologetic smile on his face. 'I need something warm and real to hold on to.'

Startled by his request, she stared at him for a moment, fingers of fear and excitement licking at her nerves. While she was almost sure he only wanted to be comforted, she also knew how shaky her own control might be in the circumstances. But her hesitation was so brief that Davin could scarcely have noticed it. He needed her and she could not say no. With a little smile of assent, she shrugged off her robe and slipped into his bed and into his waiting arms.

'Let's snuggle up spoon fashion,' he suggested, and Susanna turned, letting herself be pulled against Davin's long, hard, lean body. 'Mmmm,' he sighed contentedly, 'I feel better already.' He tucked one hand under her breasts, but made no move to go further. She could feel his breath warm against her ear, feel him gradually begin to relax, the hard tension of his limbs melt away. In a short time his breathing became the regular breathing of sleep.

I'll never be able to sleep, Susanna thought, her every sense drinking in the wonderful closeness of the man she loved. But she did not want to move and wake him. Think about something else, she ordered herself firmly. Tell yourself a story. Try *Goldilocks and the Three Bears*. Once upon a time . . . Before she got through the three bowls of porridge, she was asleep.

When she next opened her eyes, sunlight was pouring through the curtains. Somehow during the night she and Davin had reversed their positions and she was now behind him, her arm around him and her hand held firmly against his chest, her cheek against his broad back. For a few minutes as she came awake she savoured her position, her body responding quickly with unruly desires that resisted her attempts to squelch them with mental discipline. Better to leave before . . . She pulled gently on her hand, but Davin's tightened on it immediately.

'Good morning,' his deep voice said gruffly. 'I didn't want to move and wake you.' He turned over and smiled at her, and her heart nearly stopped beating at the deep desire she saw in his beautiful sea-green eyes. 'Sleep well?'

'Very,' she barely whispered. 'Did you?'

'Like a baby.' He smiled and brushed her curls back from her face, then leaned on an elbow as he bent his head to kiss her sleepy eyes, her cheeks, and then, for a long, ecstatic time, her parted lips. Susanna trembled at his touch. She wanted to reach out, to crush Davin to her, but she dared not. Instead she ran her fingers tenderly down his beard-roughened cheek, trying to tell him with her lips all that was in her heart. Did he understand? she wondered as he sighed deeply and gave her a warmly affectionate smile.

'Wonderful way to wake up,' he said softly, playing his hand through her curls and kissing her again. Then he drew back with a rueful grimace. 'I think I'd better head for the shower,' he said, and quickly turned and slipped out of the far side of the bed, leaving Susanna feeling as tense and empty and alone as if she had been abandoned on an ice floe, her body aching and on fire with longing.

'Damn you, Davin Sigmundsen,' she muttered under her breath at his retreating back. 'I don't know about you, but I can't take much more of this frustration.

One of these days I'm going to out-and-out assault you!'

Feeling decidedly cross, she got to her feet, looking over at her own still neatly made bed. 'Next time he wants something warm to cuddle I'll get him an electric teddy bear,' she groused, 'or a plain old hot water bottle.'

There was the sound of a splash from the pool and Olga's voice calling out, 'Keep your feet together!' Bobby was already up and active, and the knowledge jolted Susanna out of her funk and reminded her of the very good reasons she had spent the night in Davin's arms. 'Oh, well, I guess I'll live,' she sighed, deciding that a nice cool dip in the pool might calm her feverish body. She slipped into a plain yellow one-piece suit, brushed her hair, found her cover-up and a big towel and was out on the pool deck before Davin had ceased his loud singing in the shower. Calling a cheery 'Good morning!' to Olga and Bobby, she dropped her things on a lounge chair and dived neatly into the deep end of the pool.

Davin came and joined Olga by the pool, watching as Susanna and Bobby dived and swam a little longer. Then Olga called the maid to bring their breakfast to the large, umbrella-shaded table where she sat.

'No point in dripping all over the house,' she said with a smile. 'Now tell me, what do you young folks have planned for this week?'

'Well,' said Davin with a grin at Bobby, 'I have tickets for the Raiders' exhibition game next Sunday, we're going out with Hank on Saturday, Friday there's a baseball game, and besides that the options are the zoo, Marineland, surfing, Disneyland. I'm not going in to the store unless there's a real emergency. It's up to you,

Champ,' he said to the boy, whose eyes had grown wider and wider at Davin's recitation.

'All of them,' he said eagerly.

'That's what I was afraid you'd say,' Davin said dryly, with a wink for Susanna. 'Next week I can recuperate and Susanna can get you outfitted for school.'

By Friday night Susanna's feet were as tired as if she had run several marathons, for keeping up with Davin's long-legged stride kept her at a jog most of the time. She was bruised from falling from her surfboard, and her voice was hoarse from squealing at the rides at Disneyland and alternately cheering and yelling at the umpires at the ball game. But her happiness at being so definitely included by Davin in all the activities more than made up for her discomfort. She was delighted by Davin too. Bobby's manic excitement had gradually wound down, thanks in no small part to Davin's expert handling; he instinctively knew when to let the boy go and when to be firm. No father could have done better, she thought, as he sent Bobby off to bed early on Friday in preparation for rising at dawn to go out on Hank's fishing trawler.

'I'm turning in too,' she said with a grimace. 'I'm a wreck.'

'You can stay home tomorrow if you want,' said Davin, but his face was a picture of disappointment.

'Not on your life,' Susanna said firmly. 'I wouldn't miss that expedition for anything. Besides,' she added with a teasing grin, 'I can't let an old fossil like you outdo me!'

The following morning, bundled in heavy sweaters against the damp chill of dawn on the ocean, they boarded Hank's boat, the young man who was Hank's 'crew' immediately getting under way while Hank fixed them a hearty breakfast in the cosy cabin. Bobby was still yawning and unusually quiet, but he came to life like a shot when the anchor was dropped and fishing activities began. They used deep sea equipment, Hank having abandoned his commercial activities for the day. Davin and Bobby hooked into flounder and halibut, but all Susanna caught was a small hammerhead shark. When the sun finally broke through the coastal fog she put her pole aside and stretched out contentedly in a deck chair to watch the others. A short time later Hank came to sit beside her.

'How's life with the big fellow going?' he asked directly.

'Very well,' she answered, her conservative answer prompted by the fact that she remembered that Davin had said that Hank 'knew the whole story'.

'Just very well?' Hank persisted. He turned quizzical eyes on her, his leathery face wrinkled in a knowing smile.

'You've obviously formed your own conclusions.' She gave him a brief smile and then looked back at Davin's broad back, his head bent towards Bobby as he leaned against the rail. 'I guess "very well" is pretty inadequate,' she admitted.

'I thought as much when he called to say he'd be bringing you along.' Hank shook his head at her questioning look. 'He didn't say anything else. You'll just have to be patient for a while longer, I'm afraid.'

Susanna looked away from Hank's friendly but penetrating eyes, her heart racing. Was Hank trying to tell her in a roundabout way that Davin was going to make their marriage permanent? How could he tell? Still . . . he had easily seen how she felt. Was she that obvious, or was he that shrewd?

'It can't be easy,' Hank went on sympathetically, 'for either of you. But it's going to get better, I can tell.'

Susanna looked back at the gentle, weatherworn face of Davin's old friend and sighed. It was kind of him to try to encourage her.

'Thanks, Hank,' she said softly.

'Davin says you and Bobby have really taken to each other,' he went on. 'I'm real glad about that.'

'He's a wonderful boy,' Susanna replied. 'So much like Davin. Did you know Davin's brother? He just never talks about him, and I've wondered . . .'

'Carl?' Hank's mouth twisted wryly. 'Yeah, I knew him.'

'What was he like?'

'Everything Davin isn't. Egotistical, selfish . . . liked to flaunt his money and power. A real all-American jerk. He and Davin never got along.'

'Good heavens!' Susanna leaned forward, staring at him in surprise. 'How could they be so different?'

'Well, for one thing, they had different mothers. Carl's mother was some German baroness their old man married in an off moment. She skiied off an Alp when Carl was just a baby. I've heard he was always a brat, but maybe it wasn't his fault. I don't know the details— maybe Davin's mother didn't treat him right. That's kind of hard to believe, though. She was a fine woman.'

Susanna rubbed her chin thoughtfully and looked over at Hank, her mind now seething with questions. Apparently anticipating that, he got to his feet, giving her a sly wink.

'I've probably said too much already,' he said, then ambled off to join Davin and Bobby at the ship's rail.

'Oh, my!' breathed Susanna, gripping the arms of her chair tightly as she leaned back, her mind focusing on the possible implications of Hank's revelation. It was obvious that Bobby looked enough like Davin to be his son, but . . . no, he couldn't have been hinting at that. Just because Carl had a different mother, it didn't necessarily mean he looked very different from Davin. Susanna had seen pictures of Davin's father and grandfather, and the resemblance was striking, the dominance of that particular genetic heritage very evident. Still . . . Hank was not the sort to chatter idly . . . about anything.

Fishing was abandoned during the heat of midday, but as evening approached it picked up again and Susanna landed her first real catch of the day, a large halibut, which almost pulled her into the sea before Davin came to her rescue. Back in port, they all went to the Fish House for dinner. It was late, and Hank insisted that the bartender fix them several rounds of his speciality, the Fisherman's Delight. They were a little strong for Susanna, and she was giggling like a silly schoolgirl as Davin helped her into the car.

'Oughta call those the Fisherman's Revenge,' she mumbled, as she laid her head on Davin's shoulder and promptly fell asleep.

At home, Davin carried the soundly sleeping Bobby over his shoulder and steered Susanna into the house, leaving her on the couch in the living room next to Olga, who had been reading, refusing to admit she had been awaiting their return.

'I'll be back for her,' he told Olga with a grin as he carried Bobby to his room. When he returned Olga scolded him across Susanna's dozing form.

'You've worn the poor little thing out!'

'I think it was those drinks Hank bought,' said Davin, but he bent to peer into Susanna's face. 'She does look tired, though,' he admitted in worried tones.

'Not tired,' mumbled Susanna. 'Jus' fine.'

'Maybe you ought to skip the football game tomorrow,' Davin suggested.

'Oh, no, can't do that. I *love* football. I like baseball, I like fishing, but I *love* football.' Susanna peered through half-open eyes at Davin's face, bent close to hers.

'Okay, sport,' he said agreeably. 'Come on, off to bed now. Put your arms around my neck.'

Susanna complied with a contented sigh as he scooped her into his arms and carried her off, with a 'Good night, Olga,' over his shoulder to that amused lady, who chuckled to herself as she watched them go.

Davin set Susanna on her bed.

'Can you take your clothes off?' he asked.

In response, or lack of it, she flopped back against the pillows with a groan, her eyes closed.

'You're worse than Bobby,' Davin said, smiling to himself. He unbuttoned her thick cardigan and proceeded to undress her, receiving only minimal cooperation in response to his gentle orders to raise her arm or lift her bottom. She gave a contented, 'Mmmm,' when, unable to resist caressing her bare form, he softly stroked her and kissed her rounded, rosy-cheeked breasts.

'Want to snuggle again tonight?' he asked, his lips next to her ear. He took her answering sigh and another 'Mmmm' to mean yes, so he undressed, turned out the light, and gathered her close to him in his own bed, his own sleep gladly disturbed by the silken soft body nestled against him.

Susanna awoke next day to find Davin standing over her, dressed in his swimsuit and towelling his hair vigorously.

'How did I get here?' she asked, as she became aware of her surroundings. She also became aware that she was only half covered, and she quickly pulled up the sheet as he grinned mischievously.

'You seemed agreeable,' he said with a throaty chuckle.

'I think you took advantage of my condition,' she pouted, the throbbing of her head reminding her of the previous night.

'I didn't take advantage of you, though,' he said quickly.

More's the pity, Susanna thought, her own body stirring rapidly to wide awake desire at the sight of Davin's long-legged, broad-shouldered body standing before her. 'I didn't think you had,' she said with a grimace, followed by an impish smile. A feeling of devilment took over as her heart began pounding more loudly than her head and her longing to plunge headlong into Davin's arms grew stronger. She remembered Hank's encouraging words and boldly sat up and let go of the sheet. 'Come here,' she coaxed, waggling a finger in a beckoning manner.

'Oh, no,' said Davin, his eyebrows raised, whether in real or mock surprise Susanna was not sure. He picked up her robe and tossed it on the bed. 'It's after eleven. You'd better get a move on if we're going to get to the game on time.'

'Oh, all right,' she sighed with exaggerated reluctance, a spirit of mischief still invading her unsettled form. It was a spirit she usually kept under control, but in her just-awakened state she was taking delight in causing Davin a little of the frustration she was feeling herself. She got out of bed, picked up the robe, but did not put it on. 'It's a little late for modesty,' she said tartly, tossing the robe over her shoulder as she strolled in a hip-swinging walk towards the bathroom.

'Susanna, behave yourself,' Davin said warningly.

She turned and stuck out her tongue, then ran off laughing as he threw his towel at her. This has the makings of a really fun day, she thought to herself as she danced beneath the shower, tingling with unsuppressed excitement. Davin had been so right: she did like to live dangerously.

It did turn out to be a wonderful day, clear and sunny, not a bit of the famous Los Angeles smog to impede the brightness. It was as if the weather reflected the intensity of the awareness between Susanna and Davin, an intensity that built until every little touch between them was like a shock of electricity.

One of us is going to crack pretty soon, Susanna thought later, but she was not surprised when Davin retreated to his study that evening. Either he was not ready yet, or he was determined it would not be him that did so. She remembered Hank's admonition to be patient. Had he really meant that Davin would come to her when he was ready? What was he basing his opinion on—the simple fact that Davin had decided to take her along on the fishing trip? That really wasn't much to go on, but then . . . Hank had known Davin for a long time.

'Ever hopeful, ever patient,' Susanna muttered glumly as she brushed her hair before the mirror. 'But I never really planned to be a saint!'

CHAPTER NINE

'THAT must be quite a book,' Olga commented one warm mid-September afternoon as she seated herself beside the umbrella table where Susanna had been sitting for some time. 'You've had your nose in it for hours. What is it?'

'*The Passionate Pauper*,' answered Susanna, holding the book up for Olga to see. 'It's about a young woman who builds herself a fabulous cosmetics business but squanders most of her money on unworthy men before she finally finds the right one. I thought it might be just another gummy romance, but it's quite good. The girl is believable, not just a wooden doll.' She put the book down and stretched her legs out in front of her. 'Speaking of wooden dolls, I'm beginning to feel like one. I didn't realise I'd been sitting still for so long.'

'You've been reading a lot lately during the day,' Olga commented. 'Is that a habit, or are you getting a little bored when both of your men are away?'

'A little bored, I'm afraid,' Susanna admitted. 'I was thinking of taking some dance classes or something. That's a skill I need to improve on.'

Boredom was not her only problem. Davin's behaviour once again perplexed her. Since the night after the football game he had been, apparently, much less driven by desire, going to bed and to sleep with no difficulty. On the other hand he seemed content to let her take over the rôle of mother to Bobby, relying on her to get him started in his new school. Had she done something wrong . . . or something right? She often caught Davin watching her, his face serious but not cold or withdrawn. Was he making some decision? What would it be? She felt suspended out of time, waiting and wondering.

'Dance classes sound like a good idea,' said Olga. She gave Susanna a sly little smile. 'I may have found a little something to keep you busy, too.'

'Really? What's that?' Given Olga's resources, Susanna expected almost anything in reply.

'Actually, I may have got a bit carried away,' Olga said, looking down at her jewelled hands, her smile still mysterious, 'but you would be so perfect for the part . . .' She fixed twinkling blue eyes on Susanna. 'I volunteered you to play Alice in *Alice in Wonderland* in the Children's Home benefit play during Thanksgiving vacation. Mamie VanHooten thought you'd be perfect too. I hope you don't mind.'

'Mind? I'd love it,' Susanna said happily. 'That's one of my favourite stories. But aren't I a little tall and buxom for Alice?'

'No problem,' smiled Olga. 'We'll flatten you out a bit, and I'll just design the sets to make you look smaller.'

'Olga!' Susanna fairly squealed. 'Are you doing the sets? How marvellous!'

'I do them every year,' Olga replied. 'That's another one of those things that I do that I don't do.' She lifted her eyebrows meaningfully.

'Oh, yes,' Susanna nodded. Davin's strange quirk again. Surely he could get over that and acknowledge Olga for the still remarkable artist that she was? Maybe if she had a talk with him . . . She asked Olga more questions about the play, but her mind was still on

Davin. If only she knew more about his past and Bobby's she might be able to help him; her logic and intuition both told her there was something important there that she should know. When a momentary silence fell she chewed her lip, then asked in a carefully matter-of-fact voice.

'Olga, I've been wanting to find out more about Bobby's parents, especially his mother, but the subject doesn't seem to come up. I've been waiting for a convenient opening, but . . .' She shrugged and looked hopefully at Olga.

Olga gave her a penetrating look. 'I can imagine you must be curious,' she said. She looked into the distance, thoughtful, but rather sad. 'Elena . . . she was a beautiful girl. As a matter of fact, she looked quite a lot like Margo Fanchon.' She raised her eyebrows questioningly as Susanna gave a gasp of surprise, then went on when Susanna shook her head, not wanting to interrupt Olga's story. 'Elena was a very talented artist. When she was studying art she used to model for the classes to help pay for her tuition. She had that dark, gypsy beauty and a stunning figure. There were many men who fell under her spell. She'd had a successful showing of her paintings, but the glitter of the movies was irresistible, as it is to many girls. Carl encouraged it. With his connections . . . well, he quite swept her away with promises he couldn't keep. They each had different motives for their marriage, neither very noble, I'm afraid. It was not a happy marriage, and Bobby suffered the most from their quarrelling. If it hadn't been for Davin . . .' Her voice trailed off and she sighed heavily.

Susanna's nails were digging into her palms as she tried to maintain her surface calm while the picture of Davin's past began to form before her. There was just one other thing that she needed to know.

'There certainly isn't much of Bobby's mother in his appearance, is there?' she commented innocently. 'He and Davin look so much alike. Davin and Carl must have looked as alike as twins.'

Olga's eyes narrowed, and Susanna realised she had not been fooled by her indirect approach. 'Actually,' Olga began, but suddenly she closed her mouth momentarily and rearranged her features into a softly pleasant smile. 'Here comes our fifth grader now,' she said, raising her hand to give a jewel-sparkled wave to her great-grandson as he burst through the kitchen door with a large cookie in one hand and some papers in the other.

For a moment Susanna continued to stare at Olga, wondering what she had been about to say, but a growing certainty in her heart. Then her attention was diverted, for Bobby was upon them, waving his papers in front of them.

'The teacher let me stay after school and do some extra art work today,' he announced, enthusiasm animating every word. 'We had a special man in today who showed us how to draw horses. Look!' He held out a picture towards each of the women.

'Very good, *very* good indeed,' Olga said approvingly.

'So is this,' Susanna agreed. The picture Bobby had handed her was of a horse running free in a fancifully vivid setting that suggested desert and mountains and wildly beautiful sunsets. 'This horse looks like he's really galloping. Whenever I've tried to draw one, it looks like a barrel on stilts. How did you do it?'

Bobby shrugged, but his face was flushed with pleasure at their praise. 'It's easy. I draw horses a lot, anyway, but what the man showed us helped.'

'You like to draw and paint?' asked Susanna, thinking of the talent that came to him from his mother, and also from his father's side of the family.

'More than anything,' Bobby said seriously. 'When I get older I want to be a real artist. I want to draw real horses and maybe even go to the jungles and paint the wild animals there . . . I'd like to paint elephants and zebras and . . .' He stopped suddenly and looked up, the colour draining from his face, his eyes growing wide and frightened. Davin had come up so silently that no one had noticed, and was staring at the picture that Susanna held with a look of utter loathing, his mouth drawn down into a forbidding line and his eyes dark and cold as Arctic depths.

'Give me that!' he snarled as he reached over and snatched the picture from Susanna's shaking hand. 'You'd better get those foolish notions out of your head once and for all, young man,' he grated in a voice so harsh that Susanna shuddered. He looked briefly at the picture, ripped it to shreds, and flung the pieces violently into the pool. 'There are far better things for a man to do in this world than paint pictures,' he went on, grasping Bobby's chin in his hand and staring into his face as if he were looking at something far beyond the real world. 'I absolutely forbid you to waste your time in such a manner. Is that clear?'

Bobby's face was ashen, tears welling up in his eyes. He made no move to nod, or even to answer, and as Susanna watched in horror she felt white-hot anger rising within her. What kind of madness was this? How dared Davin appear on the scene like some avenging angel, railing at Bobby for his innocent interest in art? Only a monumental effort kept her from jumping to her feet and shouting out her comments on Davin's utterly unreasonable demand. Only her concern that the boy should not witness a terrible fight between herself and Davin kept her silent, waiting watchfully as Davin continued his probing stare to which Bobby remained as unresponsive as stone. Finally Davin dropped his hand.

'Remember what I said,' he growled, then turned on his heel and left the group by the pool, disappearing, stiff-backed, into the door to his study.

As soon as he had gone, Susanna stood and put her arms around Bobby. 'We seem to have a bit of a problem, don't we?' she said with a gentle smile, brushing the tears from his cheeks. 'I know Davin sounds terribly unreasonable right now, but he's not an unreasonable man. I'll have to talk with him—I'm sure he'll come around.'

'No!' Bobby jerked his head from side to side. 'He'll just get mad at you, too. Don't have a fight, please don't.' He looked pleadingly at her. 'I don't have to paint any more.' His face was flushed and blotchy now, tears running down his cheeks.

Susanna pulled him close, her cheek against his damp one. His whole thin young body, almost as tall as her own, was rigid with unhappiness. 'Don't worry,' she said comfortingly, 'Davin and I won't have a fight. And you won't have to stop painting, I promise you. Just have a little confidence in me, okay?' She drew back and smiled encouragingly at him.

Bobby stared at her sweet, calm face, his eyes still welling with tears. 'You won't have a fight?' he choked out.

Susanna shook her head, her heart aching at what the boy's question revealed.

'You'll still love Uncle Davin?' Bobby persisted.

A huge lump came into Susanna's throat. What on

earth could she do but say it? She nodded as she forced the lump away. 'Of course I will,' she said softly. 'I'll always love him.'

Bobby wiped away his tears with the back of his hand, a young pair of sea-green eyes now beginning to clear again. He flung his arms around her impulsively. 'I love you, Susanna,' he said, as she hugged him back, unable to speak lest she too begin to cry.

'I love you too, Bobby,' she finally managed to say, tears sparkling on her lashes. 'And so does Davin—very, very much. And don't you ever forget it.'

'I won't,' Bobby said soberly.

Olga, who had been watching the scene, her own eyes suspiciously misty, now spoke up. 'I think Bobby and I should have a game of Scrabble before dinner. How about it, young man? Go and wash your face and then come on down to my apartment. I plan to use my big dictionary this time, since you're getting so good at it.'

'Good idea,' Susanna seconded, and Bobby smiled, perceiving the diversion.

'Okay,' he agreed, 'if I can use your big dictionary too.'

'Certainly,' nodded Olga. 'That's only fair.'

As Bobby disappeared, she rose and smiled at Susanna. 'You handled that beautifully,' she said, 'but are you sure you can deliver on that promise? You've taken on quite a challenge, perhaps more than you know.'

'I have to try,' Susanna said simply. 'And I think I understand the problem, even though I don't know all the details. Perhaps it's better that way.' She turned to go, then stopped, turning again to look at Olga. 'Did Davin and Carl look alike?'

Olga shook her head. 'Not at all. Carl was short

and fair and not especially handsome.' She looked at Susanna questioningly and Susanna nodded, her virtual certainty now confirmed.

She went swiftly to the sliding door to her bedroom, slipping inside and watching until she saw Bobby and Olga go off together towards the far end of the house. At least if she and Davin did have a shouting match they would be well out of earshot, she thought grimly, as she turned to go to beard her tiger in his lair.

She again half expected to find the door to the study locked, but it was not, and she entered quietly and shut the door behind her. Davin was sitting at his desk, a glass of brandy between his hands, staring sightlessly ahead. It was impossible for Susanna to feel any anger towards him, as her eyes wandered sadly over his slumped shoulders, his down-turned mouth, the defeated droop to his usually proudly held head. She could only guess at the demon memories that were reeling themselves off before his inturned eyes, memories of a carefree young artist and his love for a beautiful, wild girl, their thoughtless passion, its bitter harvest. She could guess at most of the story now, but could not tell Davin that she knew. She could only attempt to offer him wise counsel, support, and . . . yes, love, if not explicitly then at least implicit in her tenderness and understanding. Her nervousness disappeared in her desire to comfort Davin, and she moved softly to his side. He still seemed not to notice her presence, as he turned the glass around in his hands. His shirt was open at the throat, his sleeves rolled up revealing his muscular forearms, tense as if for combat.

With one gentle hand, Susanna brushed the heavy lock of hair back from his forehead and leaned over to place her lips against his brow, her hand caressing on across his head and down inside the collar of his shirt, reaching over to enclose his taut shoulder as her other hand slid down his arm and closed over his hand. For a moment he seemed to stiffen as if in anger and then, very slowly, he let go of the glass and placed his other hand on top of hers. When he did so, Susanna bent so that she could look into his face, and very gradually his haunted eyes focused on hers.

'How about looking forward now, instead of back?' she suggested softly. 'I know you have bitter memories about art and artists—I can only guess at what they are. But Bobby needs you now. You mustn't let the past drive a wedge between you.'

Davin made no response, his eyes narrowing as he looked away across the room again. Susanna straightened, her hand still resting on his shoulder as she looked down at him. His teeth were clenched, the muscles of his jaw working, as if he were fighting some terrible battle within himself. Without looking up at her, he reached his hand up to take hold of hers as it lay on his shoulder. He pulled her towards him, and his other arm reached around her to indicate that he wanted her to sit down on his lap as he pushed his chair back from the desk. Silently Susanna did so, and immediately she was engulfed in his tight embrace, her face buried against his neck as he rubbed his cheek against her hair and his hands caressed her as if he were feeling to be sure she were real. For a long time nothing was said, then Davin asked in a hoarse whisper,

'Why am I such a fool? Why can't I forget?'

'Perhaps . . . if you talked about it?' Susanna suggested tentatively.

Davin shifted her so that he could look into her face, his turbulent eyes searching hers for understanding.

Finally, as if satisfied that what he sought was present, he began, very slowly,

'I once spent every waking hour painting . . . drawing . . . studying art. We all planned to be great, my friends and I. All Wyeths or Picassos . . . at least. We were such typical young Bohemians, with our long hair and shabby clothes, our consuming passions and radical opinions. We lived and breathed for our "art".' He gave a short, bitter laugh. 'It's hard to remember what it was like to be so young and naïve.' He paused and took a deep breath, seeking Susanna's eyes again.

'Go on,' she said softly, and he did, staring past her now as if at a vision.

'There was a girl . . . so beautiful, so talented, so fiercely dedicated. I worshipped her, and I was overwhelmed when she fell in love with me. We made wonderful plans to spend our lives pursuing the purest of art, travelling the world together to see the great masterpieces and paint our hearts out.' Davin's mouth drew into a tight line as he stopped, the agony still hauntingly present in his beautiful eyes.

'Elena?' she breathed, afraid to ask but more afraid to let him retreat from his tale.

Davin closed his eyes momentarily and nodded. 'I was so sure, in spite of her fiery temper and her wild ways, that I'd found the one woman in the world for me. I was so sure she felt the same about me.' He gave that rasping laugh again. 'She was even pregnant with our child.' He looked directly at Susanna then, and she nodded.

'Bobby,' she said softly.

'Yes.' The word came out as a sigh. 'I never dreamed she would leave me then. It all happened so fast. We were planning our wedding one day and Carl came by . . . two weeks later they were married. He only wanted her because she was mine. She couldn't resist the glamorous life he promised her. For a while I thought I would die . . . that it couldn't be possible to live on with such pain.'

'Oh, Davin!' Susanna caressed his cheek gently, and his eyes softened at her touch.

'It sounds rather melodramatic, doesn't it? But that was the way I felt then. I abandoned art and everything that would remind me of Elena thinking, foolishly, that I could become someone else myself by doing so. It hasn't worked very well, I'm afraid.' Lines of sorrow gathered about his eyes again. 'Why would I think it would work with Bobby? Why would I ever want it to?' With a groan, he crushed Susanna to him again, a sound like a sob escaping from his throat. 'Will he ever forgive me?' he choked out hoarsely.

She raised her head and looked into those beautiful sea-green eyes that she loved so dearly. 'Of course he will—he loves you so much. All you have to do is ask. Of course,' she added with a little smile, 'I know that won't be easy.'

Davin smiled wryly. 'Easier than letting him think I hate him for being what he is. Easier than . . . explaining to him about . . . the other.'

'Perhaps,' she said meditatively, 'one thing at a time?'

'That's probably best,' he agreed. 'I do so want to find the right words so that he'll understand . . . to protect his mother's memory as much as possible. I've gone over it in my mind so often since he's been here, but . . .' He paused, frowning unhappily.

'I don't think you need to worry about that too much.' Susanna gave him a warm, confident smile. 'Bobby won't think the less of either you or Elena for having loved each other so much. He's a fine, intelligent boy.

I'm quite sure he already suspects the truth. He may only be waiting to hear it from you.'

'Just as you were?' There was a little smile in Davin's eyes now, a little light returning, as she nodded. 'I wouldn't be surprised,' he said, reaching out with one hand to touch her cheek. He bent his head and kissed her forehead, her fluttering eyelids, her cheeks, the tip of her nose, and then, very tenderly, her lips.

'Thank you, Susanna,' he said as he raised his head again. 'I seem to have to say that a lot.'

'Any time,' she replied, her heart pounding with love and the relief of almost unbearable tension. At last, she felt, Davin was on his way to solving his terrible conflict. Soon, too, he would find the way to tell Bobby, and they would become father and son, as they so obviously should be.

Very carefully, Davin set her on her feet and stood up, stretching as if to throw off some great weight, then straightening his shoulders and raising his head, his expression now strong and determined.

'I think I'd better sort out today's problem right away,' he said firmly. 'Is Bobby in his room?'

Susanna shook her head. 'No, he's playing Scrabble with Olga in her apartment.'

He nodded and started towards the door, then stopped and turned, holding out his arm to her. 'Come with me?' he asked, and smiled as she came to his side.

Olga and Bobby looked up expectantly as Davin and Susanna came into Olga's sitting room, their arms around each other. Quickly assessing Susanna's flushed and happy look, Olga smiled knowingly. Bobby remained motionless, suspended between anxiety and the desire to run into Davin's outstretched arms.

'Forgive me?' asked Davin in a low voice. 'I was

wrong.' He barely had time to brace himself against Bobby's onslaught, which was directed as much at Susanna as himself, and for a time all three were indiscriminately hugging one another.

'You'd better mark this day on your calendar, young man,' Olga said dryly from the sidelines.

At this both Susanna and Davin laughed and Bobby looked questioning.

'I think,' Susanna explained with a smile, 'that what Olga means is that there won't be too many occasions when you hear Davin admit that he was wrong about something. Of course,' she added archly, 'he hardly ever will be. Right?'

'Hardly ever,' Davin agreed, and bent swiftly to kiss her smiling mouth.

After dinner, he encouraged Bobby to bring out his pictures, and praised his efforts warmly, making helpful suggestions and then joining in with some sketches of his own as they sat at the big work table in the kitchen. In between sketches he looked at Susanna, his eyes so bright with triumph that her heart almost burst with happiness, her eyes misting with tears of joy. It was a special night for Davin, and he plainly felt deeply grateful for her part in it. For her part, Susanna was overwhelmed with a love and desire so deep that she felt shaken loose from the earth, as diaphanous as cobwebs in the wind. She drank in the warmth and strength of the man she loved until she was on fire with it, worshipping every strand of his thick, dark red hair, adoring the sculptured lines of his high cheekbones, the lush curves of his curling lashes. She adored his courage and goodness, the beauty and skill which he demonstrated as he took up again the long discarded tools of the art which he had once loved. He looked over at her as she sat watching him, her face aglow with the loving warmth of her thoughts, his eyes travelling over her face like a caress, dark with an intensity she had never seen there before.

'Shall I go to bed now?' Bobby asked softly as Davin and Susanna stared at each other across the table, the current between them almost tangible. He received a nod and a wink from his great-grandmother, who silently rose and accompanied him towards his room.

'Good night, Bobby,' Davin and Susanna said in unison as their startled eyes perceived that they were being abandoned.

Davin looked back at Susanna, and her heart leaped into her throat at the turbulence and yearning she saw both in his eyes and in the softness of his features and his parted lips. Then, very deliberately, he looked down and gathered up the papers and pencils into a neat pile. 'I guess I'd better go and tend to a little business,' he said gruffly.

'Oh, no! Don't go,' she pleaded. She could not bear it if he retreated to his study tonight. She hurried around the table to his side. 'Please. Draw something just for me.' She sat down and gazed up at him, her eyes vivid blue pools of longing.

He flicked a quick glance through his lashes at her. He took her hand, placed it palm down on the top sheet of paper, then traced around it with a pencil. 'There,' he said, shooting another brief glance at her, the corners of his mouth attempting a smile.

'You know that's not what I mean,' Susanna said in a voice harsh with frustration, edged with tears of despair that were coming closer and closer.

'I know,' Davin sighed. He picked up her slender hand and carried it to his lips, kissing the palm with lips that sent a message of unmistakable passion as he held her hand there for several seconds before he lowered it again, still enfolded in his own. He looked at her more directly. 'Shall we try some chess?' he suggested.

It was not what Susanna's not-so-secret heart had hoped for, but it was better than the earlier alternative. 'All right,' she croaked out hoarsely, following him down the long hall to his study and wondering bitterly if perhaps Job hadn't had a relatively easy time of it. She sat down at the table where Davin kept his beautiful hand-carved chess set and began arranging her pieces with clammy, trembling hands, studiously avoiding looking up at Davin as he did the same. She watched, her head bowed, as his hands slowly put his pieces in order. He set up the back row and then began lining up his pawns, one at a time, very deliberately pausing after each one as if it required a great decision to perform the simple operation. He had only two left to put in their places when suddenly his huge hand swept across the board, sending the priceless pieces flying.

'To hell with chess!' he growled, as Susanna looked up at him, startled. In one swift, fluid movement he was beside her and scooped her up from her chair, crushing her against his chest as if he were afraid she would try to flee. 'Susanna, Susanna,' he breathed over and over, his lips against her hair, as he carried her towards their room.

She clung to him, burrowed against him, drinking in his warmth and strength, her heart pounding so wildly that she was sure it would burst. At last, at last, her heart beat out the cadence. At long last she would soon belong to this man who owned her heart.

He laid her on his bed and she stretched like a jungle

cat against him, her arms tightening as he pressed his long, hard length against her, his mouth covering hers now with blinding passion, plunging into her inner softness as if he were starved for her taste. With eager throaty cries Susanna responded, grasping at his shoulders, her head reeling with fleeting bits of thoughts that were masked by sensations so heady that no sense could come from their skittering fragments. Touching and being touched, to drown in sensations of closeness, were all that mattered. She tugged Davin's shirt free, her hands eager, tender messengers of love as she wonderingly explored the soft mat of hair on his chest, and drew silken little fingers across the smoothly muscled planes of his back. Her action triggered his, his eyes flaming emeralds of joy and desire that caressed her face, as with incredible gentleness he unfastened her blouse and cupped her breast in his hand. She trembled violently as he lowered his head to tantalise first one rosy nipple and then the other.

'Oh, Davin,' she moaned softly, as she felt her body flower into openness. She clutched his shoulders to hold him there, never wanting the ecstasy to stop and at the same time aching for that final fulfilment she had never known. As if the strength of her grasp were nothing, Davin pulled back, gazing at her with eyes dark and slumbrous with longing, yet deeply serious.

'I want you so desperately,' he whispered hoarsely. 'Are you sure this is what you want too?' He was motionless, not breathing or moving, while tears of love for this good and infinitely thoughtful man blurred her starry eyes.

'Oh, yes, Davin, yes!' she answered.

His smile glowed, his arms tightened, his eager hips pressed against her. He threw one long leg across her, then groaned through lips that nuzzled her ear, 'Too many clothes.'

Susanna laughed with sheer delight as he stood and stripped off his clothes, her skin on fire with tingling anticipation, her own fingers clumsy as she sought to remove her clothing. How beautiful he is, she thought, knowing that it was true beauty that she saw in the perfection of his masculine form.

Davin lowered himself beside her again, his shining eyes sea-green depths into which she gladly fell as she moved against him, revelling in the feeling of touching the rough warmth of his body with every inch of her own, every sensation adding to the building tension, carrying her higher into clouds far beyond any ever seen from earth, where the air was filled with softness, where silken sheets became silver rivers of cool delight and simple lamplight burst into rainbows. Large, long-fingered hands caressed the peach-soft skin of her back and the womanly curves below while, with lips that kissed and nibbled gently and a tongue that tantalised, Davin blazed an unforgettable trail across peaks and valleys, not stopping until she cried out and reached to pull him back above her, to have him fill the need that had become all-consuming. With delicate care he responded, slowly at first and then, as she arched with abandon to meet his thrusts, with an eagerness that matched her own, two becoming as one as they rushed along with the raging torrent they had so long denied. When at last they reached the wildly beautiful end of their journey Susanna heard, as if from afar, her cries of ecstasy, tears of happiness coming to her eyes at Davin's look of joy and contentment as he, too, found release and groaned with satisfaction.

'So beautiful,' she whispered in wonder, her limbs

feeling light and soft and ethereal as she slowly floated down from the dizzying heights they had shared.

'Yes,' Davin murmured, 'it was.' Still holding her as if she were a treasure that might slip from his grasp, he moved beside her, sighing deeply as she nestled against him, her cheek buried against his shoulder. Together they drifted off to sleep, drugged by the aftermath of their passion.

CHAPTER TEN

WHEN Susanna awakened from her deep, contented sleep she reached out to touch Davin and found that she was alone. It was early daylight, pale and colourless and suddenly bleak. Where had he gone? A delayed sense of guilt washed over her as vivid images of the passion she and Davin had shared came back to her like a recurring dream. She had done exactly what she had once promised herself she would not do, even though as time passed she had realised the difficulty of keeping that promise. Neither of them had spoken of love . . . they had spoken only of desire . . . and now Davin had left her alone. Had he, too, been filled with guilt and regret? Had he been shocked to find her a virgin, horrified that she might now expect him to remain bound by their marriage vows? Or had he felt her love for him, did he feel love for her, too? Had they only failed to communicate on this most important fact?

She sat up, rubbing her sleepy eyes. She would have to have a talk with Davin, make him understand . . . Leaning her chin on her hand and frowning, she sighed deeply. How can I tell him that I want him for ever, but if he doesn't want me that way then I don't? she thought in miserable confusion.

The door to the bathroom clicked open and Davin came through, dressed in a deep brown turtle-neck sweater and beige slacks. It was not his usual apparel for a day at the store, Susanna thought, but he looked magnificent anyway. He could never look anything but magnificent.

'Good morning,' said Davin with a little smile, although his eyes remained serious and a frown traced a small line between his brows. 'Did you sleep well?'

It was a rather formal greeting, considering the circumstances, Susanna thought, and her heart sank. Something was obviously bothering Davin. 'Just fine,' she answered in a thin voice.

'That's good. I was thinking . . .' he began, then looked away for a moment and started again. 'I was thinking that perhaps we ought to discuss . . . extending our contract.' He got the words out this time, but as if with an effort.

'Oh, no!' she cried out reflexively, as her worst fears were realised. 'I mean, you don't have to . . . just because of last night. That is, I want to discuss it . . . if you want to, but I don't . . . I don't want you to feel that . . . I mean, I can still go back to . . . I still *want* to . . .' She stopped, looking pleadingly at him. How on earth could she tell Davin what she wanted to tell him without him feeling in some measure obliged to keep her on with him even though it might not be what he wanted? He had such a strong sense of duty . . . towards Bobby, the Winters, Olga. He could never bear for anyone to suffer the rejection he had once felt. How easily it might lead him to take on a lifelong obligation to her.

'Could we talk about it later?' Susanna asked anxiously. 'I don't seem to be expressing myself very well.'

'I think I know what you're trying to say.' Davin's eyes were smiling now.

'No, I don't think you do.' She lifted worried eyes to his.

'We'll see.' He put on his suede sports jacket. 'I'm going to Futura today,' he said, explaining his different garb. 'Olga's been asking me to look into some things over there for quite a while, and I think I'm ready to tackle it now. Since it's Friday, I thought I'd pay them a surprise visit and let them know I'll be needing an office there starting next week.' He bent and brushed Susanna's cheek with his lips. 'Don't look so worried,' he said gently. 'Everything's going to work out.' He gave her a reassuring smile and then turned and left the room.

She watched him go, her heart thumping dismally. There was no way Davin could have understood what she really wanted to say from the garbled mass of words she had emitted. What had he thought she meant? She frowned to herself as she dragged herself out of bed and into the shower. What was this business about Futura? Did that have anything to do with her? She kept puzzling about it as she dressed in jeans and a sweater, having no plans to do anything all day except try to figure out how she could communicate the right things to Davin. The more she thought about it, the more she thought Davin must have thought she *hated* the idea of being married to him for more than a year. She at least must get that notion out of his head.

The day dragged on, Susanna finding no answer to her dilemma that seemed suitable. She was dozing by the pool when the maid brought her the telephone.

'Mr Sigmundsen to speak to you, ma'am,' she said, and Susanna's heart flipped over as she thanked the woman and took the phone.

'Hello?' she answered, realising it was ridiculous for her to sound as timid and tentative as she did. She pulled herself together with an effort. 'How are things at Futura?'

'They're in a state of shock at my sudden appearance,'

Davin said dryly. 'You've never seen so many people running around like chickens with their heads off!'

'It will probably do them good,' Susanna replied. 'Everyone needs shaking up now and then. What can I do for you?'

'Come to a party with me tonight. It's at Cyril's, which I know you won't enjoy, but I think we ought to be there. There'll be some people there I want to see.'

'Formal?' she asked.

'No. Wear that black cocktail dress. I won't have time to come home, so have Jarl bring you to the store to meet me. And bring along one of my dark suits and a shirt and tie, will you?' he added. 'Meet me at six. We'll have dinner and then go on to the party.'

'Sure thing,' Susanna said brightly, although she found the whole business rather mystifying. What could have happened to have Davin so eager to go to the party at such short notice?

The atmosphere at the party did nothing to clarify questions. Cyril was obsequiously friendly, oozing out compliments about Susanna's appearance, pretending delight at Davin's renewed interest in Futura, although his eyes darted anxiously about the room as he sought to keep track of where Davin was and with whom. He introduced Susanna to the new 'light of his life', Janna Montrose, a starlet whom Susanna had known slightly in the past as a girl with far more bosom than talent.

'I wonder if he promised to make Janna a great star,' she whispered to Davin later.

'It probably only took a bit part to get her,' Davin replied cynically. He was surveying the room with cold eyes; it was apparent that he had not come to this party for fun.

After everyone had had a few drinks, Susanna was

bemused to find that more and more people came up to her, beaming as if she were a long-lost friend. She found herself on the receiving end of curious questions that seemed to be sidling up to the point the questioner really wanted to address. 'I think Futura is really going to go places in the next few years, don't you?' What on earth did that mean? 'I expect the European influence is just what we've been needing, don't you?' European influence? Susanna replied in vague generalities and noticed that the questioners' eyes narrowed speculatively, as if wondering what she was keeping from them. Or perhaps it was what they were keeping from her, she thought suddenly, as across the room she saw the tiny form of Margo Fanchon, who had apparently just arrived. She watched with clenched teeth as Cyril fawned over the woman, nodded in response to a question . . . then led her directly to Davin's side.

Her tension grew as she saw Davin greet Margo with a Continental kiss of her hand, his face lighting up as if he were finally ready to enjoy the party. Then he draped his arm around her and they went off together into an adjacent room, and closed the door behind them.

For more than an hour, Davin was closeted with Margo. Over and over Susanna surreptitiously glanced from her watch to the closed door. She was scarcely aware of the people around her, drifting from one group to another, smiling and nodding as if she knew what they were talking about, but unable to remember a word anyone said. Then, suddenly, Davin was back at her side.

'Sorry I neglected you for so long,' he said with a perfunctory nod. 'You remember Margo, don't you?'

'Yes, of course.' Susanna flashed the woman a brief but brilliant smile. 'How are you?' It was impossible to miss the fact that Margo was very well indeed, her cheeks flushed and her eyes suspiciously bright.

'Getting better, I think,' said Margo with a conspiratorial glance at Davin from under thick black lashes. 'Your husband is a very persuasive man.'

They chatted for a while, then took their leave. As Davin started the Ferrari he remarked, 'That went better than I'd expected. Did you have a good time?'

'Oh, yes, fine,' Susanna lied. 'I was a little miffed, though, that you spent so much time with Margo.' No use letting him think she'd enjoyed that part of it, she thought sulkily.

'Sorry about that,' said Davin, patting her knee absently. 'I had a proposition to make to her. I think she just may be the answer to our problem.'

At Davin's words Susanna's heart plummeted into her stomach and she had a terrible urge to cry out in sheer pain. He had once made a 'proposition' to her. Was he making a similar one to Margo, already lining up someone to take her place on a more permanent basis? Margo had been married, but maybe that was on the rocks by now. Or maybe she was willing to change partners if Davin was available and pressed his case. Oh, yes, Davin was persuasive all right. How well she knew! Feeling utterly sick and miserable, Susanna stared silently out at the damp, smoggy night, hardly noticing that Davin was silent too as she fought to keep from bursting into sobs that would reveal to him how much she had hoped that their prearranged ending would never come to pass.

When they arrived at Davin's home, he seemed not to notice Susanna's gloomy expression. He reached into the back of the car and took out a huge pile of thick, official-looking books, his face bearing the abstracted look of someone whose mind is far away.

'Damn stuff should have been on computers long ago,' he grumbled as he carried the pile into the house. He paused briefly at the door to their bedroom, taking note of Susanna's pale face for the first time. 'You look tired,' he said gruffly. 'Sorry that party was such a drag. I've got to look at these damn books tonight, so I won't be going to bed for a while.' He pecked at her cheek. 'Sleep well.'

She nodded numbly. 'Don't work too hard,' she said, making her lips curve in an imitation of a smile, then escaping to the blessed peace of their room, where she flung herself on her bed and sobbed uncontrollably.

After a long night of soul-searching, Susanna had regained most of her composure. All her problems were of her own making, she reasoned, and she would just have to be strong and make the best of things no matter how bad she might feel. She would give Davin no cause to complain that she was not carrying out her bargain. It was only too apparent that their one night of passion had warned him that things were getting out of hand, and he had decided to begin preparing for the inevitable change. It still was possible that he had mistaken what she said for a denial of any interest in prolonging their relationship, but there was no way now that she was going to set him straight, for if he had thought so it had obviously not disturbed him. Instead he had gone straight to work to find her replacement . . . his old flame, Margo Fanchon. At least he was consistent, he had to be given credit for that! For how many years had he pined over Elena, rejecting everything to do with artists just because she had apparently thrown her impetuous young lover over for his brother, Carl, even though she was pregnant with his child? Consistent was too mild a word. Stuck in a rut was more like it! Just as he was stuck in a rut now, unable to give up their silly scheme even though it should be quite apparent to him that she was everything that he and Bobby needed. Well, Susanna Blair was not going to be that way. Somehow she would get through the rest of her year or however long she was needed, and then go on to other things. She had advised Davin to look forward instead of back; she would take her own advice.

Susanna was assisted in her grim determination to make the best of things by Olga, whose plans for *Alice in Wonderland* were taking shape and required a meeting that very afternoon. Davin was nowhere to be seen, and in response to Susanna's question about his absence Olga replied that he had gone to see some lawyers, and had taken Bobby to spend the day with Hank, 'So we won't have to bother about him.'

Is he already trying to separate us? Susanna wondered with a pang of sorrow. She was at least reassured on that point, for the trip they had planned to the zoo the next day so that Bobby could draw the animals was not cancelled, even though Davin was still engaged in some mysterious activities involving frequent telephone calls. He looked tired and distraught, but wished Bobby and Susanna a good time as they prepared to leave.

'Sorry I can't come,' he said, giving Susanna a friendly hug and a kiss that sent her heart racing in spite of her feeble efforts to resist her automatic response to this man who still owned her heart. 'I've found a lot more going on at Futura than I bargained for.'

He had frequent cause to wonder what it was that he had found, for during the next couple of weeks he was seldom at home, and when he was his face was clouded with a grim look. He managed at times to be warm and affectionate with both her and Bobby, taking great interest in the myriad paintings the boy now showed him and praising Susanna for the way she was filling in for him in his absence, but whenever his attention was not required he lapsed into a brooding silence that filled his surroundings with a cloud of gloom.

Nothing more was said about Margo Fanchon. Whatever Davin had found at Futura, it must have taken precedence over his plans with Margo, Susanna reasoned. Some contrary part of her mind hoped Futura would keep him busy for a very long time, defying the logic that told her such hopes would only prolong her agony. Thank goodness that between her new dance classes and working on the play and taking care of Bobby she was too busy to have much time to fret.

The rest of October fled by, Susanna frequently having the feeling that she was trying to catch up with it. She felt more and more like the White Rabbit, rather than Alice, with a touch of the Mad Hatter thrown in. She was tempted to skip her dance classes, especially when she was called out of one to come to the school and pick up Bobby, who had come down with a 'flu virus. Olga relied on her to badger the people who were working on the sets, to keep at anyone who was behind schedule to get cracking. The director had all but retired in favour of Susanna, who was able with a combination of tact and demonstration to get very creditable performances out of the volunteer actors.

Davin worked longer and longer hours on whatever mysterious business was going on at Futura, trying valiantly to keep up with his store as well. On the first day of November he came home early.

'Are you finally going to take an evening off?' asked Susanna, looking anxiously at his drawn, pale face. He had lost weight, his prominent cheekbones making him look almost haggard.

'I'm afraid not,' he replied, taking her by the arm. 'Come on in the bedroom with me—I've got to pack.'

'Pack? Where are you going?' she asked as he hurried her along.

'San Francisco, Houston, Dallas, New York, Paris, London,' Davin reeled off in rapid succession. 'And anywhere else that seems useful.' He shut the bedroom door behind them, tossed his bulging brief case onto the bed, and opened it. 'Have you read this?' he asked, thrusting a copy of *The Passionate Pauper* towards her.

'Yes,' she answered, 'but I don't understand. Why . . .'

'In a minute, in a minute,' he said impatiently. 'Can you imagine Janna Montrose as the heroine?' he asked, gesturing with the book, his voice a low growl.

'Good lord, no,' she answered, her eyes widening. 'Is she going to do that?'

'Heaven forbid!' Davin replied. He pulled a thick manuscript from his briefcase. 'This is the proposed screenplay. It stinks. It was written for Janna by guess who?'

'Cyril? You mean he really did promise her something like that?'

'So it seems,' he shrugged, his lips curling in disgust. 'The damn fool. I'm not sure he could write one even if he didn't have some ulterior motive in mind. I want you to do me a favour while I'm gone. Rewrite it, with yourself in mind as the heroine.'

Susanna stood stock still, staring at him. 'Are you kidding? I've never written a screenplay! I mean, I have some idea how to go about it, but . . .' She turned her head to follow Davin as he retrieved a suitcase from his closet and placed it on the bed, flipping it open.

'I know,' he said over his shoulder, 'but you might as well give it a try. I haven't found anything yet you couldn't do. Just read over that mess of Cyril's and see if anything can be salvaged, then go on from there.'

'But . . .' Susanna felt a wave of anxiety, 'I've got the play right now—I won't have much time for a while. How long have I got on the screenplay?'

'Oh, six months anyway. No rush. I just want to see what you can do with it by the time I get back.' He continued tossing clothes into his suitcase, finally pushing it shut and fastening it as he heaved a heavy sigh. He sank down wearily on the edge of the bed, his head in his hands.

It was more than Susanna could resist. She sat down beside him and began to massage his tense neck and shoulders. 'Mmmm,' he groaned in pleasure, 'keep that up and I may never leave!'

Oh, how I wish you never would, Susanna thought, longing to hold him close, to kiss him until they both forgot the world around them once more. She knew she must not give in to her impulse, but she did press her cheek against his, revelling for one brief moment in the touch of his skin and the scent of his familiar aftershave. 'I . . . we'll miss you,' she said softly.

'I'll miss you too,' said Davin, a deep, mysterious yearning in the cloudy depths of sea-green that were his eyes. He pulled her on to his lap, holding her close against him, burying his face against her hair. 'I wouldn't go, except the entire mess is my fault, indirectly. I'll explain it all to you when I get back. If everything works out as I hope it will . . . I think I'll have some good news for you then.'

'How long will you be gone?' asked Susanna, the lump in her throat making her voice husky. Was he going to finally tell her about his future plans when he returned? He might think it would be good news, but it was something she never wanted to hear, she thought, burrowing closer against his strong chest.

'I don't know. Two or three weeks, maybe longer. I'll keep you posted. I hate to dump all the responsibility for Bobby on you like this, but I know I can count on you to do the right thing, and it will only be this one time, I promise you that.'

'I don't mind,' Susanna said softly. 'Bobby and I get along beautifully.'

Davin nodded. 'I know. If only . . .' He paused and shook his head. 'It can't be helped,' he muttered, almost to himself. Then he set her on her feet and stood up himself, straightening his drooping shoulders with an effort. 'I've made a list of a few things that need attention while I'm gone.' He fumbled in his briefcase again and handed her a paper. 'Mostly it's just routine stuff around the house. The only thing out of the ordinary is that dinner at the Harmons' in two weeks. I'd like you to go to it even if I'm not back. Just keep your ears open and let me know what you hear.'

Susanna stared blankly at the list in her hand. She had a strange feeling of being shifted into a new role, without really knowing what the rules were or how she was to play the part. She wanted to clutch at Davin's arm, beg him to tell her more, but her sixth sense warned her that it would be useless and that he did not need any extra badgering at the moment. Instead she managed a bright smile. 'I'll do my best,' she answered, and was rewarded with a grateful smile in return.

'Good girl!' Davin picked up his suitcase. 'I'll say goodbye to Bobby and Olga now,' he said. He looked at Susanna, still standing motionless, her list in her hand, then he put the suitcase down again and came to stand in front of her, lifting her chin with his hand. 'I wish I could be more specific . . . about a lot of things,' he said, his eyes troubled, 'but it's best if I'm not right now. If everything works out the way I hope, I'm sure you'll like the results.' With a quick kiss, he was gone.

CHAPTER ELEVEN

'YOU'D do anything to please that grandson of mine, wouldn't you?' said Olga almost two weeks later, as she surveyed Susanna's pale face and dark-circled eyes with pursed mouthed disapproval.

The truth of that statement made Susanna fidget uncomfortably under Olga's concerned gaze. She had tried to deny it, tried to convince herself that she was really going forward into new and interesting adventures as she worked late night after night on the screenplay Davin had assigned her. Deep inside she knew better. It was the only thing that kept her from going crazy with loneliness and longing for Davin's presence at night after Bobby and Olga had retired. Even now she denied the truth of Olga's statement.

'I . . . I've never written anything before,' she said defensively. 'It's exciting. I just can't seem to stop once I get started.'

'You'd better learn to stop,' Olga said tartly. 'You're going to collapse like a punctured balloon if you don't get more rest. The way you look we'll have to call the play *Alice in Zombieland*.'

'Yes, ma'am,' Susanna said contritely, for she had looked in the mirror and knew Olga was not exaggerating. Still, when Davin called from New York that next night she was glad that she could report significant progress on the screenplay.

'I'll be going to the Harmons' tomorrow night,' she said brightly, after Davin had complimented her on her diligence. 'Where shall I call to make my report?'

'Better let me call you on Sunday,' Davin replied. 'I'll be flying to London tomorrow and I don't know yet where I'll be staying. I may luck out and stay with friends instead of a hotel. Give Bobby my love, and have fun at the Harmons' if you can.'

The next evening as Susanna dressed for the party she remembered Davin's words 'if you can' and felt a qualm of anxiety. Why was she not supposed to enjoy herself? Was it going to be another strange evening with people prying for information she did not have?

The occasion of the party was the fortieth wedding anniversary of Cory Harmon and his wife. Cory was a retired member of the board of Futura, and the event was true Hollywood style, with lavish decorations of huge paper wedding bells, poster-size blow-ups of the Harmons' wedding pictures, and fountains of pink champagne bubbling in the foyer of the chic restaurant. After leaving her chinchilla with an attendant, Susanna picked up a glass of champagne and began to circulate among the guests, some of whom she knew from the studio. She went up to a group of people with whom she had worked on *Murder for Fun*.

'Hello, Bill,' she said to the assistant producer.

'Hello,' he said coldly, deliberately turning his back on her.

That was strange, Susanna thought; they had never had any problems before. She approached some women she had known on the set. Their conversation stopped as she came nearer, their frosty stares making her feel as welcome as a leper. She veered away after a brief hello. The same scenario was repeated over and over. At first Susanna was angry, then curious. Davin had told her to keep her ears open, so she wandered about between groups trying to catch bits of the various conversations. What she heard made little sense: 'Poor Cyril,' she heard more than once, as well as 'Sigmundsen's crazy!' One man said grimly, 'We'll all go together.' She was trying to puzzle it out when she almost ran into 'poor Cyril'.

'Well, well,' he said, focusing his beady eyes on her in his usual offensive manner, 'I didn't expect to see you here, Susanna. Having a good time?'

'Not especially,' she replied icily, attempting to push past him.

Cyril chuckled nastily and grasped her arm in his clammy fingers. 'I've been watching how everyone shuns you,' he murmured, breathing heavily in her ear. 'It's quite entertaining, really, but I gather it's all a mystery to you.' He chuckled again as she gave him a stony stare. 'You really don't have the slightest idea what your husband is up to, do you?' There was a look of wicked triumph in his eyes as he repeated, 'Not the slightest idea. How delightful!' He dropped her arm and backed away, his mouth smiling below the cold slits of his eyes.

More baffled than ever, Susanna retreated to the powder room, her contact with Cyril and the other strange events having made her stomach feel dangerously queasy. While she was in one of the booths she heard the click of heels as two more women entered, one of them laughing merrily.

'I don't think it's such a joke,' the other woman said in a soft voice. 'Really, how would you like to wake up some morning and read in the papers how your husband had been chasing some woman halfway around the world.'

'Oh, but she should have known,' the higher voice responded silkily. 'Davin Sigmundsen is too hot a property for some poor little starlet. Margo Fanchon is definitely more his speed. They've had a thing going for years, I've heard.'

'That's just gossip,' the second voice chided. 'But I suppose there might be more to it this time. This time he might have Margo and save Futura at the same time. Not a bad combination.'

'Sort of like having your cake and eating it too?' the first voice asked with a giggle.

'That sounds positively vulgar, darling,' the second voice said with a nervous titter, 'but I like it.'

Heels clicked again and the door closed, leaving Susanna frozen in silent despair, unseen and unheard, the crushing knot in her stomach and the leaden ache in her heart so painful that she dared not move lest she collapse on the floor.

'I must get out of here, I must go home,' she breathed, trying to regain enough calm to do so without faltering. 'I will not fall apart here, I will not.' She fought down the waves of nausea that swept over her, fastened her mind clearly on the one task at hand, to escape, and then marched firmly out of the powder room, picked up her coat from the check room, and ordered her car from the doorman.

Jarl took one look at Susanna's ashen face and quickly bundled her into the car, covering her with a warm blanket. By the time they were home, Susanna had regained her composure enough to wave off Jarl's assistance.

'I'm all right now,' she said to the anxious old man. 'Really I am. It was just something I ate that didn't set quite right. Please don't say anything to Olga—I don't want her to worry.' With a bright smile she swept past him into the house, into her room, and flung herself, sobbing, onto her bed.

By morning, Susanna had cried out all her tears and sanity had returned. Two nights of crying were more than enough, she told herself grimly. Davin had given her a clue himself. She should not have been so shocked by Cyril's innuendo or the women's gossip. But hope, even false hope, dies hard. There was no point in blaming Davin, either. The message he had got the morning after their passionate lovemaking must have been that it had meant nothing to her, that she did not want any extension of their contract, that she only wanted to go back to her career as soon as possible. Now Davin was trying to help by bringing the one woman he had loved in the years between Elena and now back into his life. A woman, Olga had said, very like Elena. How would Bobby take to her? For both their sakes she hoped it would be love at first sight, for nothing in the world could make her wish anything but happiness for Bobby. Then another thought occurred to her: perhaps Margo already knew Bobby. Perhaps she even knew that he was Davin's son. 'What a tangled web,' Susanna thought sadly. 'I'm sure Bobby must wonder why he looks like his uncle instead of his supposed father.' Why had Davin still not told him the truth? How long could that deception go on?

One fact from the disastrous evening still bore into Susanna's mind and, as if compelled by some diabolical force, she went in search of the previous day's newspaper. She found it and hurried back to her room, quickly flipping through the pages until she came to the gossip columns, then scanning down the columns until she found what she was seeking:

'DAVIN SIGMUNDSEN may have found the perfect answer to settling the suit which Margo Fanchon has been pursuing against Futura Pictures. If you can't beat 'em, join 'em—eh, Davin?'

Susanna reread the item several times, wondering when the reaction would set in. Nothing happened. It was as if she were suddenly immune to any shocks, the news registering with a mechanical series of clicks like a long-distance telephone connection. Yes, she remembered now that there had been a legal suit. It had something to do with a profit-sharing agreement that Margo had signed when a TV mini-series she had starred in was produced under the auspices of Futura. Margo's lawyers must have really got their claws into Futura, Susanna mused, for hadn't one of those women remarked something about both saving Futura and getting Margo? There must have been quite a shake-up at Futura, too. That would account for those strange remarks. Poor Davin, Susanna thought charitably, now he was probably wondering how she was going to react to being booted out of her job as his wife so soon. Well, she wouldn't give him any trouble. Not if he really could arrange to star her in *The Passionate Pauper*. She could see now that he must have had something like that in mind when he gave her the script to work on. Letting her down gently, or trying to. Meanwhile, she would keep smiling and do her duty by Bobby, until Davin returned and they could make suitable arrangements for the transition that would cause that poor little lad as little pain as possible.

When Davin called, Susanna was lightly flippant about the débâcle at the Harmons' party, recounting the strange comments and telling him only that she was treated like a bad case of poison ivy. Davin's response was a growled series of epithets concerning the origins and destinations of Cyril and several others. He talked to Bobby for a while, enquired about his school work, then asked to talk to Susanna again.

'I don't know if I'll be back for your play,' he said. 'I still have to go to Paris and Rome, but I'll do my best.'

'Don't worry about it,' said Susanna quickly. 'It's just a kid's thing, you know.'

'Nonsense!' Davin sounded gruff. 'I really do want to see it. Take care now, sweetheart. I'll talk to you again soon.'

'Sweetheart!' she muttered to herself after he had hung up. My, my, but Davin was really going Hollywood! she thought. Next thing he'd be calling her darling!

Susanna floated towards the days of the play at the top speed, keyed up as if on increased voltage. Nervousness made her more hungry instead of less, as if the double existence she still felt she was living demanded a double ration of food. The costumes were finally ready only three days before the play, the traditional one of Alice having been executed by a fine seamstress so that it was a lovely masterpiece of petticoats and pale blue voile. To minimise her voluptuous curves, Susanna had to wear an elastic binding beneath her costume, and, as the seamstress wound it around her preparatory to a final try-on, she felt a sharp stab of pain in both breasts that caused her to suck in her breath suddenly.

'Are you all right?' the seamstress asked anxiously as Susanna grew pale before her eyes.

'Oh, yes,' Susanna breathed, mechanically raising her arms to put on the dress, her mind in a dither. Her breasts were occasionally tender between periods, but never anything like this. They were really painful. Wasn't that what her mother said had been her first symptom of . . . Frantically she tried to remember the date she and Davin had made love, but it had been so long ago, and since then . . .

'You've put on a little weight,' the seamstress commented, tugging at the zipper. 'Pull in your tummy, dear.'

Susanna did as instructed, then suddenly she burst into laughter before the startled seamstress, clutching her arms about herself and rocking back and forth, tears streaming down her cheeks. How absolutely hilarious it was—a pregnant *Alice in Wonderland*! She laughed on and on, sinking into a chair, her head in her hands, tears dripping on to her lovely costume. She heard the seamstress's taut voice saying 'I don't know what started it,' and Olga's deep tones, 'She's hysterical.' Then there was a sharp slap to her cheek that rocked her head back and she found herself staring up into Olga's furious countenance.

'I'll kill that grandson of mine when he gets back!' she fumed. 'Putting all that extra work on you! You've worn yourself to the point of exhaustion. I've seen it coming, but you always smile and say it's no problem to do ten things at once. I know you'd do anything for that big ox, but you'll just have to learn to say no once in a while. Now get out of that costume immediately—I'm taking you home and putting you to bed.'

'Yes, ma'am,' Susanna said meekly. She felt utterly drained, as if she could easily sleep for a week. She would get some rest, and then try to figure out what to do.

It did not take her long to reach a decision. As soon as

the play was over she would go home to Iowa. She would tell Davin that the guilt over deceiving her parents was taking too heavy a toll and that she must confess and get her life in order once again. She would not tell him about the baby until after the divorce, for there was no way she would permit the child to force him into a permanent commitment. Afterwards she would tell him, and they could work out some amicable agreement for sharing time with their child.

Her decision made, Susanna felt somewhat better. Just the idea of getting away from the brash phoneyness of Hollywood lifted her spirits, as well as the thought of returning to her own home. Christmas would soon be here, and in Iowa snow . . . real snow, not the makebelieve Hollywood kind. She made a reservation for her flight back to Iowa for the morning after the last performance of the play.

In spite of everything, the performances of *Alice* went extremely well. Susanna threw herself wholeheartedly into her part, loving the thunderous applause and the curtain calls. It was so much more fun than performing in front of a cold, lifeless camera. I'll have more fun in the Little Theater back home than I'd ever have in Hollywood, Susanna thought triumphantly. She was especially delighted at the children who came up to her and the White Rabbit and the others, their eyes big with wonder as if they were truly those characters come to life.

'You were sensational,' Olga told her after the second performance. 'I knew you'd be perfect for Alice. I certainly hope Davin shows up for the performance tomorrow.'

'Oh, so do I,' Susanna said automatically, but her nerves tingled uneasily at the thought. She had put off thinking about confronting him, dimly hoping that she might get away before he returned; it would be so much easier to leave him a letter. She squelched the thought again, comforting herself with adages about not crossing bridges and borrowing trouble.

Olga was fuming when Davin had not appeared by curtain time for the final Sunday matinee performance, but Susanna breathed a sigh of relief. She enjoyed herself once again, her cheeks pink with pleasure at the generous response of the audience, smiling and bowing and accepting a huge bouquet of roses. Then the house lights came on and she saw him. There he was, his dark red hair gleaming in the lights, smack in the middle of the front row, next to Olga. Beside him was someone small and dark . . . Margo Fanchon.

For a moment Susanna thought she was going to faint, but she clenched her teeth and regained her composure, then made her way down from the stage with the others so that the children could see the magical characters up close. She was bending over one adorable curly-headed moppet when she felt instinctively that Davin had come up behind her. Her heart pounding, she turned to face him.

'Hello, Davin,' she said tightly, willing her rubbery legs to support her. He was so tall, so handsome, those sea-green eyes still inviting her to drown in their depths. No, Susanna, not again! she warned herself.

'You were wonderful,' said Davin, bending to kiss her cheek. He placed his hands on her shoulders, but she shook him off. 'What's wrong?' he asked, his expression both shocked and surprised.

'I'll tell you at home.' Susanna gave him a perfunctory smile. 'Excuse me. My public awaits.'

She spent an inordinately long time talking to the

children who lingered in the theatre and then removing her make-up and putting on her own clothes. Her mind refused to function, the only thought she could cling to being one of getting away as quickly as possible, ending the terrible pain. Finally she had to join Olga in the limousine for the ride that, as is always the case in such circumstances, was all too short. Davin's car was already in the wide, circular driveway.

'I wonder if Margo is here,' murmured Susanna, not sure she could maintain her control and be cordial to the woman if she were.

'I think she went home with some friends,' Olga replied, removing one thorn from her path.

Dinner was a strained affair, with Susanna now the one who was stonily silent, Olga giving her grandson looks redolent with disgust as she blamed him for overworking his wife, and Davin trying valiantly to salvage the situation with bright accounts of his trip. At last it was over, and Davin clutched Susanna's arm, peering into her face as if he were looking to see where she had gone.

'Now will you talk to me?' he demanded.

'Certainly,' she replied stiffly. 'Let's go to your study.'

'Well?' he demanded as the door of the study closed behind them. He was now wearing a dark frown. 'This isn't exactly the welcome I expected,' he added, folding his arms and glaring down at Susanna.

'I'm sorry,' Susanna said, tilting her chin to look up at the towering man. 'I didn't want to tell you over the telephone.' She looked away from those compelling eyes and steeled herself before looking back. 'I'm going home to Iowa tomorrow,' she said, her voice firm and unemotional. 'I can no longer go on with our deception. It's not fair to my parents, or Bobby, or anyone. It's beginning to affect my health. I'm . . . taking medication for my stomach. It's time I stepped out of the picture and let you get ready for . . .' she could not say 'Margo' '. . . your permanent wife,' she finished.

Davin's face became colourless, his eyes blank, staring orbs. 'You're leaving? You don't even want to hear about what I accomplished on my trip, what my plans are?'

'No.' Susanna shook her head firmly. 'I already know most of the details, and I congratulate you. You seem to have achieved everything you set out to do. I've written over half of the screenplay, and I'll leave it for you to look at. If you wish me to continue, you can contact me at home.' Her every muscle ached from tension as she cast about in her mind for anything else she needed to say.

'But what about Bobby?' demanded Davin hoarsely. 'What will I tell him?'

'I'm sure you must have planned something,' Susanna replied. 'You can delay a while by just telling him I've gone home for a visit. I'll tell him that myself.' She frowned at Davin's still dumbstruck expression. 'I don't see why you're so surprised that your chickens are coming home to roost,' she said coldly, her eyes glittering and narrowed as she clung to a fierce bravado to get her through these endless moments. Perhaps now was the time to push one other issue! 'Don't you think it's time you told Bobby the truth, too, before that comes back to haunt you?'

'I'll talk to him right away . . . tonight . . . I promise,' Davin said quickly, seeing her glance towards the door. 'But, Susanna . . .' He moved towards her, reaching for her with both hands.

'Don't, Davin,' Susanna said tightly, and his hands

dropped to his sides. 'This isn't easy for me, but it's something I must do. I'm sorry it seems to be such a shock to you, but . . .' She stopped, sensing that more words were useless, and turned towards the door, then back again. 'Would you mind sleeping in here tonight? If you would, then I'll do so.'

Davin said nothing, only shaking his head, his face first utterly drained and lost looking, then losing all expression as he seemed to retreat into his shell, like a window to the world vanishing, only a wall remaining. Before she could give in to an almost overwhelming impulse to comfort him, she fled.

CHAPTER TWELVE

'THEY didn't stay in California, did they?'

'What?' asked Susanna, pretending she did not know that her mother was referring to her troubles. She had been home less than twenty-four hours and already she was regretting her sudden flight. Images of Davin's stricken face, Bobby's fearful one and Olga's shocked expression loomed before her eyes. Could she have been wrong? Her stomach churned as she surveyed the hearty breakfast her mother had put before her, and now her mother was beginning those inevitable questions.

'You know what I mean,' Mrs Blair said tartly. She sighed and her voice became more gentle. 'Is it another woman?'

Susanna looked up. 'Y-yes,' she choked out, then burst into tears. 'Please, Mother, I can't talk about it yet,' she sobbed. 'I . . . I need to rest up and think about what to do.' She mopped her face with a paper napkin and gave her mother a wounded look, knowing it was probably useless to play for sympathy. Her mother was not easily diverted.

'You've talked it out with Davin?' Mrs Blair persisted.

'Yes . . . no . . . not exactly,' mumbled Susanna.

'He's told you he prefers someone else?'

'No . . . but . . . everyone knows.'

'Oh, really?' Mrs Blair's eyebrows rose sceptically. 'And who is this "everyone"?'

'It's . . . everyone. Even the newspapers.'

'My, my! You're married to one of the best-looking men in Hollywood, head of a major studio, and you believe things like that? I'm surprised at you!'

'You don't understand!' Susanna cried. 'She's an old flame—he's known her for years. Besides . . .' She stopped, shaking and feeling nauseous. She couldn't tell her mother the whole story yet, she just couldn't. She wasn't sure . . . Besides, if she was getting little sympathy now, that would really set her mother off. Why couldn't she be a nice mother-hen type of mother that couldn't bear to see her poor little daughter wronged? Susanna thought resentfully. She had forgotten during her years away from home how her mother had verbally bludgeoned her into confessions she never planned to make, and into taking responsibility for her own actions, no matter how much she tried to dodge the blame. 'You're about as sympathetic as a . . . a tree!' Susanna grumbled, pushing her plate of food away untouched.

Mrs Blair stared at her daughter thoughtfully. 'It breaks my heart to see you so unhappy,' she said softly, 'but it would break it even more to see you make a terrible mistake.'

'I've already made one,' Susanna said miserably, not sure which one she meant.

'As much as you love Davin and he loves you? I think not,' said Mrs Blair, surveying Susanna's untouched breakfast. 'Are you pregnant?' she asked bluntly.

Susanna's eyes grew wide above their shadowed hollows. 'How . . . how . . .' she stammered.

'Not too hard,' Mrs Blair replied with a knowing smile. 'So I'm to be a grandmother.' She looked at Susanna sharply. 'You do want the child?'

'Of course!'

'It is Davin's?'

'Mother!'

'Does he know?'

Tears began pouring down Susanna's cheeks again as she shook her head. 'I . . . couldn't tell him . . . couldn't use it to . . . to hold him . . . wouldn't be fair . . .' she sobbed.

'To whom?' Mrs Blair asked softly. 'Listen to me, Susanna. I can't live your life for you, but I can tell you a little story. Once upon a time there were rumours about your father . . . after all, he was the handsomest man in three counties, still is . . . and there were so-called witnesses who did me the great favour of letting me know about his philandering. I was pregnant with Jeff at the time, but your father didn't know that, and I had some of the same feelings you're having. I didn't want to use the baby to hold a man who didn't want me. I ran home to Mother, and she gave me little sympathy, but plenty of food for thought. Why, she asked, was I giving up so easily? What made his judgment better than mine, assuming there was truth in what I'd heard? I loved him, and he had certainly acted as if he loved me. Was there nothing to salvage, nothing to talk about, nothing to do but turn tail and run? How could I think of leaving my unborn child fatherless on such skimpy evidence?' Mrs Blair paused and looked at Susanna, her blue eyes deep and thoughtful as she remembered. 'It wasn't easy, but I went back . . . thank God.'

'He . . . wasn't . . . ?'

'No. He had perfectly good explanations for what had been seen.'

Susanna shuddered, trying to imagine her own life without her wonderful father. 'I . . . don't know,' she said slowly.

'Think about it,' her mother advised, rising from her

chair. 'You can have a few days to rest now.'

Susanna got up also, feeling suddenly lighter and more free than she had in many days. 'I think I'll go for a walk,' she said, and her mother nodded. The two women exchanged a smile, and suddenly Susanna flung her arms around her mother and hugged her tightly. 'Thank you, Mommy,' she said, giving her a kiss on the cheek.

'Any time,' Mrs Blair replied, and at those words Susanna burst into joyous laughter, as her mother stared in startled surprise.

'It's just that . . . now I know where I got it!' Susanna cried. 'Never mind, I'll tell you later . . .' She grabbed her sweater and went flying out the door. Why is it, she wondered as she strode swiftly down the lane, drinking in the crisp clear air, that we never realise until it hits us right between the eyes how we got to be the way we are?

Her mood sobered as she began to think, more clearly now, about Davin and Margo and her own future. There was still that dreadful agreement, too, which made her problem different from her mother's but maybe it didn't matter that much after all. Davin had certainly acted as if he loved her, even though she had not admitted it to herself. Maybe he had been afraid to tell her for fear she, like Elena, would reject his love. Maybe those *were* just rumours. Maybe he, too, had good explanations. There were too many maybes and too few answers. She would have to go back, and soon. Davin needed her, the big ox! She thought of dear Olga, and Bobby. They needed her too. 'Shame on you, Susanna,' she scolded herself. 'You ran away without a fight!'

That night Susanna did sleep well, for the first time in many nights. In the morning she awakened and then dozed again, listening to the familiar sounds of her mother cleaning, the telephone ringing, doors opening and closing. It was quieter than when her brothers were home, and she vaguely wished they were not away at college, and then slept again. It was almost noon when there was a persistent tap on her door and her mother entered.

'Better wake up now, Sleeping Beauty,' said Mrs Blair. 'Company's coming.'

'Who?' asked Susanna, sitting up and stretching. 'I feel so much better already,' she added, smiling at her mother.

'That's good. You look better, too.' Mrs Blair smiled back, her eyes alive with a combination of mischief and delight. 'Davin's coming.'

'What!' Susanna's voice was a hoarse shout.

'Not so loud, dear, I'm not deaf. He called from O'Hare very early. He was renting a car. He should be here soon,' her mother said matter-of-factly.

Susanna stared at her mother, aghast. 'You sound like you're reading the shopping list. What did he say? Why is he coming?'

Mrs Blair chuckled. 'He didn't say much, he just wanted directions. But from the sound of his voice I'd say you're going to have some listening to do.'

'Listening! He's going to have plenty of listening to do himself!' Susanna retorted.

'Good,' said Mrs Blair with a satisfied smile. 'Have a nice fight. Your father and I are going out for a while— you won't need eavesdroppers.'

Good lord, Susanna thought as her mother left, this wasn't fair! She wasn't ready! But did the fact that Davin was coming mean . . . that he loved her? Never once had it occurred to her that he might come after her. Always before, when he had retreated into his shell, she had had to badger him out of it. She had half expected to find him, on her return, still standing like a statue where she had left him. But he was coming here . . . and soon! Like a shot, Susanna jumped from her bed and dashed into the shower, the hot spray only adding to her tingling uncertainty. In minutes she was dressed in jeans and a sweater, sipping coffee and stuffing homemade cinnamon rolls into her mouth as if she had not eaten in weeks.

Impatiently she paced to the front windows and looked out, then back to the kitchen, her agitation growing by the minute. She sat at the kitchen table again, her mind in an unproductive dither, her ears primed for the slightest sound of a car approaching. Numerous cars passed, each one sending her heart racing, but none turned into the long drive back from the road. Finally one slowed, then accelerated again towards the house. Susanna shut her eyes briefly. 'Dear God,' she prayed softly, 'please let him want me.' Then she stood and hurried towards the front door, opening it and watching as that tall, familiar man flung open his car door and strode swiftly up the walk and onto the porch.

The Davin Sigmundsen that Susanna watched approach was not the elegant, sophisticated, withdrawn man she had left. His face was unshaven and hollow-eyed with fatigue, his clothing rumpled, his mane of dark red hair tousled as if fingers had beaten a regular path through it. He stopped inches in front of her and stared at her, his eyes wild, deep-sea pools at first and then softening as he surveyed her upturned face, her parted lips, her misty eyes.

'Davin,' Susanna whispered softly, holding out her arms, then crying out in happiness as she was crushed in an embrace that almost welded her body to his. She managed to pull him inside and shut the door before his mouth possessed hers in a kiss that took her breath away, a rough cheek rubbed hers, and that wonderfully deep voice repeated over and over, 'Susanna, my darling Susanna!'

'You're not angry with me?' she got out in wonder.

'Angry? Of course not.' He looked down at her, his own eyes moist with tears. 'You're not . . . angry with me any more?'

'I never was.' Susanna clung to him, finding it difficult to remember why she had ever left him. 'I was just . . . hurt, and confused, I guess. I thought . . . you wanted someone else.'

Davin groaned. 'Poor little thing,' he said softly, crushing her to him again. He looked around the Blairs' comfortable living room and led her to the sofa, folding her carefully into his arms as he sat down. 'Margo told me how you must have felt,' he said grimly.

'Margo?'

'Yes. Margo . . . and several other people. My God, Susanna, you should have been there right after you left!' He paused and gave a short, harsh laugh. 'That would have been difficult, wouldn't it? All hell broke loose. Olga cursed me in both English and Danish, Bobby cried and wouldn't go to school, Olga called Margo and she came over and cursed me in French and Italian. You haven't lived until you've been cursed in four languages in less than an hour!' Davin smiled ruefully and kissed Susanna's nose. 'I felt like jumping off something before they started in, but by the time they were through I could have crawled through the eye of a needle.'

'They told you to come and get me?' asked Susanna, a little frown wrinkling her smooth forehead.

'They certainly did,' Davin answered. 'Amongst other things.'

'Would you have come if they hadn't?' Susanna's eyes narrowed now as she contemplated his answer.

'Uh-oh,' Davin sighed, 'I've done it again, haven't I?' He took her face between his large hands and kissed her lips, then drew back and looked at her soberly, shaking his head. 'I'm a romantic fool, Susanna, on that I'm sure you'll agree when you've heard the whole story. But I do love you, with all my heart, and I never want you to leave me. Make no mistake about that, ever again.'

Tears flooded her eyes but she blinked them back. 'I love you too,' she cried. 'I always have and I always will.'

'I know. Bobby told me. Olga told me. They were thoroughly disgusted that I wasn't sure of it. However . . .' he frowned at Susanna, '. . . it would have helped if you'd told me too.'

'I was . . . afraid,' she whispered.

'I know. So was I,' Davin said gently. 'And I'm more to blame than you. I was afraid because of Elena. You were only trying to honour that stupid agreement.'

'Stupid?' It was Susanna's turn to frown. 'When did you decide that it was stupid.'

'It always was. Have you any idea how long I had been watching you, wishing I had the courage to ask you out, to see if you were as lovely as I supposed, to let myself hope you might fall in love with me?'

Susanna shook her head, her eyes caressing his face lovingly. 'How long?'

'Over a year.'

'So instead you hired me to be your wife. That doesn't make much sense, Davin Sigmundsen. No sense at all, in fact.'

'That doesn't seem to be my speciality,' he replied dryly. 'I don't know why you put up with me.'

'Because I adore you,' said Susanna, her arms curling around Davin's neck. She nuzzled his ear. 'Is this story much longer?'

'Down, woman,' Davin said with a throaty chuckle. 'Let me finish. I concocted that plan when I found out about the Winters, after Carl and Elena were killed. It seemed to solve two problems at once, at least on the surface. I kept hoping mine would disappear, that I could really be the man you deserved, but . . .' he took Susanna's face between his hands again and kissed her lips as if they were as delicate as rose petals, 'I never would have been, without you, nor could I have been the kind of father Bobby needs.'

'Oh, Davin,' Susanna sighed, burying her face against his massive chest. 'I love Bobby so much, too—it almost killed me to leave him. Are you . . . and he . . . ?'

'Yes, we're father and son now. Good lord,' groaned Davin, his hands caressing Susanna in long, loving strokes, 'so much has happened in the last two days!'

'Tell me about it,' suggested Susanna, her own hands invading the front of his jacket and beginning to un-button his shirt. 'I must have been terribly wrong, but this time I'll be glad to hear about it.'

'You mean about Margo?' he asked, and she nodded, pushing his shirt open so that she could rub her cheek against his rough chest. 'You'd better stop that or you won't hear much,' he warned with a deep, contented groan. 'Well, you were right, in a way. I am very fond of Margo. She's the only other woman I know who can knock some sense into me when I need it. She really tore me apart for leaving you in the dark about my feelings and plans. I'd told her all about them, and when you left she immediately sensed that it was I who had failed somewhere, and in two minutes she had reduced all my reasons to ashes and left me feeling like an utter fool. You see,' Davin said, lifting Susanna's face to his with his hand, 'I wanted to be your knight in shining armour and present the world to you on a silver platter. That morning . . . after we had made love . . . I did so want to tell you how I loved you, but . . . well, what you said made me think that even though you might be willing to stay with me, you wanted to continue with your career too. I thought that was only fair. You are a very talented lady, you know.' He stopped again to kiss her, his hands stealing up inside her sweater and across her bare skin to caress her breasts very gently. 'And so,' he continued with a sigh, 'I went on my naïve mission to Futura to make sure that you would not only continue your career, but would get the kind of opportunity you deserve. What I found there was the most God-awful mess you can imagine.'

'You found that out right away?' asked Susanna, remembering that first strange party.

'I'm not considered a whiz at business for nothing,' Davin said with a crooked grin. 'And Margo helped— that's what I was talking to her about at Cyril's party. She suspected he was behind Futura's cheating of her, and it turned out he was. He and several others had been skimming the profits for years. They made the mistake of trying to convince me the business was going under and I should let them buy me out. It smelled fishy right from the start. Not only that, but Margo was going to win her suit and she and her husband . . .' Davin paused and gave her a firm frown, 'a very happy couple, could really have put Futura out of business. Instead, I convinced them to come in with me as partners, and we've put together a consortium of investors from all over the world that will make Futura the most powerful company in the industry. Cyril and his group are out and we're soon going to be ready to do some of the most exciting things the entertainment business has ever seen. And one of the first things we'll do,' he paused and nibbled deliciously at her lips, 'is a first-rate production of *The Passionate Pauper*, with *your* screenplay and . . . the same fantastic lady as the star.'

Susanna stared up at Davin's triumphant face, her mouth pursed into a line that spoke volumes of aggravation. 'Now *that* explains that item in the paper! Why in the world didn't you tell me what was going on? It would have saved so much trouble.' She gasped as he pushed her sweater up and gently took one of her rosy nipples into his mouth.

'Is there a bed in this house?' he asked, raising his head and giving her an innocent smile.

'You're not answering me,' Susanna warned, her heart pounding as he gave his attention to her other breast with devastating effect.

'In a way I am,' he replied, his eyes dark with love as he looked into her face once more. 'I loved you so much, wanted you so much, that I had to try to make everything perfect before I told you. I was so afraid . . .'

Susanna's heart caught as even now she saw the darkness cross Davin's face. 'The shadow of Elena,' she said softly, her hand reaching out to caress his rough cheek.

He nodded. 'I guess you know enough of the story. She wanted me in bed, but that was all, even when she found she was going to have our child. After that I was never sure of any woman's love.'

'You can be sure of mine,' Susanna said quickly. 'I was

coming back, very soon, to try to talk some sense into you if you were really thinking about Margo as my replacement.'

'I never was,' Davin assured her. 'Never. I don't know what you heard, but it's only gossip. I'm afraid it won't ever go away.'

'That's what my mother said,' she sighed. She moved her lips across his chin and up to his mouth. 'I'll tell you where to find a bed now,' she murmured against his lips, 'if you're still interested.'

'How long will we be alone?' he asked, gathering her into his arms. 'This may take a while.'

'Don't worry,' Susanna chuckled softly. 'My parents will understand.' She directed him to her room, and together they shared a new kind of joy, making love at the beginning of a lifetime together.

'There's just one other thing you ought to know,' Susanna said later, as she lay stretched contentedly against Davin's warm, bare skin.

'What's that?' he asked, idly tracing figures around her breasts and across her abdomen with his finger.

'I may not want to make that movie for a while.'

'Oh? Why not? It would be perfect . . .' Davin's voice trailed off as he followed her eyes towards her rounded tummy, already not as flat as it once had been. He looked back at her face, his eyes bright as emeralds, his mouth opening and then spreading into a wide smile. 'You're not . . . you are!' he cried as she nodded. He looked again at her stomach and then back into her eyes, tears sparkling in his and his whole body trembling as he took her into his arms and held her close as if she were fragile as a cobweb. 'Good lord,' he muttered hoarsely, 'and I almost lost you.'

'No, you didn't,' Susanna said firmly. 'You would

have had one very devil of the time getting rid of me.'
She hugged him close, changing his tentative embrace
to one that was strong and yet infinitely tender. There
was the sound of a door opening and closing. 'I think
Grandma and Grandpa have returned,' she murmured
against Davin's ear.

'They know?'

'Mother guessed. I'm sure she's told Dad.'

Davin released her slowly and got to his feet. 'I think
we should call Great-Great-Grandmother and Bobby,'
he said. 'They wanted to come along and make sure I
didn't botch things up again. Will they be surprised!' He
looked around Susanna's cosy room. 'Are you sure
you're ready to go back to California? It's so peaceful
here.'

'Oh, yes,' she replied, coming up behind him and
putting her arms around him. 'Wherever you are, that's
where I belong.'

Davin turned and encircled her with his arms. 'Till
death us do part,' he said softly. 'I meant it then, you
know.'

'So did I,' said Susanna, her eyes bright as the happiness that swelled within her. 'So did I!'